Hot Coco

An Unbridled Adventure

BY

Cindy McDonald

Hot Coco

For information call: 304-285-8205
or Email: cindys.mcdonald@gmail.com

Designed by Acorn Book Services

Publication Managed by Acorn Book Services
www.acornbookservices.com
info@acornbookservices.com
304-285-8205

ISBN-10: 0985726717
ISBN-13: 978-0-9857267-1-3

Printed in the United States of America

For my husband, Bill, thank you for your loving support always.
You are my best friend and the love of my life.

Acknowledgements

There are many people I wish to thank that had a hand in the publishing and pre-publishing process of *Hot Coco*. I wish to thank three women who so enthusiastically encouraged me to move forward with this project, Janet Oellig; Cynthia Schoettker; and, my dear friend, Linda Taylor.

Thanks to my wonderful publishing manager and fellow author Lauren Carr for her constant support and insightful editing; and the creative genius behind this fabulous cover, Todd Aune. Thank you to those at Acorn Book Services that worked behind-the-scenes on my behalf.

Last, but certainly never least; I want to thank my husband Saint Bill, who has always supported me in everything that I have done—the dance school, and now my writing. Your love and understanding knows no bounds. Thank you.

TABLE OF CONTENTS

"Be yourself; everyone else is already taken."

-Oscar Wilde

Hot Coco

Part One

Too Hot to Handle

Cindy McDonald

~ *One* ~

The early morning mist cradled Keystone Downs Thoroughbred Racetrack. In the not so far distance the wispy pines snuggled in against the Allegheny Mountains, which rose out of the haze like Christmas trees after a downy white snowfall. The sun's golden beams glimmered through the ashen vapors to warm the old tin roofs of the long shed rows that housed the horses on the back side of the Thoroughbred racetrack. Pigeons nesting on the roofs warbled. Horse trailers would bang while pulling into the barn area. Exercise riders called out greetings in Spanish to one and other, as the pumped-up Thoroughbred's hooves *clop, clop, clopped* against the pavement on their way to the track for their morning workouts.

Keystone Downs had awakened to meet a new day.

Punch McMinn toted two buckets to the door of Westwood Stables and emptied them into the roadway. A huge black man, he was the size of a Pittsburgh Steelers linebacker. His physique gave him a daunting appearance, but the simple truth was Punch McMinn was nothing more than a softy. He cared for sick kittens in the barn; he was a sucker for stray dogs; and, of course, he administered TLC to the racehorses with the gentleness of velvet, even though his hands were large and callused.

Punch handled his many hats with a kindhearted finesse. He had been the stable manager for Westwood Thoroughbred Farm for many years. Having grown-up with the younger generation of the

West family, he oftentimes was a confidant; a big brother; and, yes, sometimes a therapist.

Humming along with the stable radio, he dumped the contents of the second bucket into the roadway when the sound of hooves pounding fast and furious against the pavement caused him to hesitate and look up into the heavy fog.

Riders called frantically at each other, "*Salga del camino!*" *Get out of the way.*

Suddenly, four Thoroughbreds materialized through the mist to gallop freely through the shed row. Steam burst from their nostrils. Their eyes were wild with excitement and their manes tossed in the air. Sucking himself against the wall, Punch strained to see riders jumping from their mounts to pull them aside while the rouge renegades thundered past.

His tubby tummy bouncing up and down, a fat Mexican stable hand ambled behind the loose horses while calling out in Spanish for the horses to come back.

A tall, reed-thin young man named Scott Carter was also chasing after the escapees. He cleaned stalls and cooled-out horses for Doug O'Conner, one of the trainers. His sapphire eyes were kind and his rugged jaw line was sharp. Unlike most of the track tramps that appeared out of nowhere to work only long enough to collect what little money they could for booze or a fix, Scott was semi-educated and polite.

Bringing up the rear was the crusty old horse trainer, Doug O'Conner. A sour-faced man, he had no use for a kind word or a gentle tone. His personal comfort was at the forefront of his priorities. His track uniform consisted of a pair of pajama pants, an old T-shirt, and beat-up slippers. His dark gray hair was always in need of a stiff combing, and he shaved when he damned well got around to it.

"Need some help, Doug?" Punch called out to the old fart.

"Go to hell, McMinn," he roughly retorted. He wasn't joking.

"You're welcome." With a shake of his head, Punch retreated back into the barn.

 CB ED CB ED

The haze was beginning to dissipate when Mike West pulled his truck into the track parking lot. He yawned into his fist, stretched his back before he turned off the ignition, and slid from the driver's seat. The truck expelled a deep *beep, beep*, when he pressed the lock button on the key ring.

When he turned toward the barn area, his eyes were drawn to a tall, leggy, blonde bombshell. She was the equal to any *Playboy* centerfold. His eyebrow arched and the left side of his mouth curved upward.

With a bucket filled with oats, the lovely woman was coaxing a grey Thoroughbred. Interested in what she had to offer, the horse inched toward her until he came almost within her grasp. The closer the Thoroughbred came, the more her blue eyes brightened and her plump lips curled in anticipation.

Mike couldn't deny such a beautiful damsel in distress. So, he sauntered toward her and her four-legged friend to assist in any way he could.

The Thoroughbred stretched his nose toward the bucket to sniff the sweet oats smothered in molasses. The blonde's eyes grew wider. Cautiously, she reached out her hand to grab the horse's halter.

The ornery equine jerked his head up. His nose caught on the very edge of the bucket, flipped it into the air, and then he bolted in the opposite direction.

The blonde grappled for the spinning bucket and the sticky oats that were flying all around until it landed on Mike's head. Cupping her hand over her mouth, she gasped.

Staggering around like a poor imitation of a tight rope walker, Mike tried to pull the bucket from his head. The molasses-drenched oats dripped down his neck and over his shoulders.

When she reached for the bucket, her feet became tangled which caused her to tumble into Mike and knock him to the ground. When he finally managed to yank the bucket from his head, Mike found himself nose-to-nose with the beautiful blonde, who was straddling him.

Other than the oats clinging to his hair and clothes, he'd been in worse positions.

"Are you all right?" she asked while gasping for breath.

A bit dazed, he nodded.

Losing all composure, her eyes welled up with tears. "I can't catch my horse," she cried, "and my trainer dumped me. I don't know what to do." Sobbing uncontrollably, she pulled out a tissue and forcibly blew her red nose into it.

Mike brushed some of the icky oats from his shoulder and gently lifted the overwhelmed beauty from his body. "Calm down. Who's your trainer?"

She studied his square jaw that accentuated his ruggedly handsome face. His dark shaggy hair was littered with oats and molasses. His blue T-shirt swept over his broad shoulders and clung to his tightly sculpted torso that eased into his lean hips. Wiping the tears from her cheeks, she peeked at him from the top of her wet eyes.

"Doug O'Conner." She sniffed. "He's a very mean man. I paid him good money. I'll just find myself another trainer." She pitched Mike a coquettish glance and softened her voice. "Do you know any?"

"A few, I'm Mike West, and you are …"

"Coco … Coco Beardmore." She offered him her hand.

Making a fascinating connection, he shook it.

Beardmore was a well-known name in Pennsylvania. One of the top employers in the Lanzville and Rosemount area, Beardmore Industries made the non-glare screens for all the major computer companies. The Beardmores were one of the wealthiest families in Pennsylvania—Hell, the wealthiest family east of the Mississippi.

Mike went for it. "Beardmore … of Beardmore Industries?"

Her eyes brightened. "Yes, my father owns the company."

All of a sudden, it was no effort to come up with an available trainer for the lovely Miss Coco Beardmore.

"Hey Mike, we're ready to go. You coming?" Shane's voice snapped Mike's cunning train of thought. His younger brother strolled toward him with a mouthful of doughnut, and grape jelly filling drizzling on his chin.

Coco's eyes took a quick tour of Shane West's muscled physique, his sandy hair, square jaw line, and crystal blue eyes. Walking towards her, he was all flash and swagger. He put one thought in mind: *Here comes a player.*

Tossing the doughnut into a trash barrel, Shane moved in for a closer look at the blonde.

Wincing, Mike pointed to the jelly on his chin. With a coy shrug, his brother wiped it away. "This is Coco Beardmore. This is Shane."

She continued to smile while Shane scanned.

Mike told him, "Coco needs a new training stable."

Immersed in making the hot blonde/big boobs connection, Shane wasn't making the Beardmore/Beardmore Industries connection. He stepped in closer. "Well, hel-lo, Co-co."

"Are you a trainer?" she asked in a smooth tone.

"Yep."

Mike stepped in front of the youngest and most impetuous West. "Uh, he's an assistant trainer. I'm actually the head trainer."

"Mmmm, how lucky can I get?"

"We need to retrieve Coco's horses from Doug O'Conner's barn," he told Shane before turning to her. "How many are there?"

"Five." She hiked up her chin with pride. "Five very well-bred horses."

"Doug O'Conner?" Shane snorted. "Oh, yeah, this ought to be fun."

ೞ ಐ ಚ ಐ

Doug O'Conner's disposition had become down-right unbearable. The sweat poured from his forehead, and matted his grungy gray hair to his scalp. Swearing under his breath through the large brown wad of snuff that bulged from his lower lip, he wiped down one of the Thoroughbreds that had been among the wild and free earlier that morning.

Scott held and stroked the nervous horse while Doug's dirty old rag mopped the sweaty lather from its hide.

"I'm telling you, Coco's bad-luck, boy," he said. "I'm sick and tired of the headaches and damages her horses cause. Shit, I spend half my day fixing what they've tore-up."

"Maybe you should raise your training fees, and make Coco pay for the damages. Or you could pawn her off on someone else," Scott suggested.

Doug scowled at him over the horse's back. "I'll think on it." He glanced around the unkempt, old stable until he spotted his homely browbeaten daughter cleaning a nearby stall. "Margie, fetch me a bucket of fresh water," he bellowed.

Pushing an overloaded wheelbarrow, Margie emerged from the stall. Her dingy brunette hair was pulled back from her gaunt face that was too small for her nose. Her right front tooth folded over the left one. She wore a faded flannel shirt that had belonged to her father over her oversized, stained T-shirt, and dirty jeans.

In contrast to her nose and teeth, her almond-shaped eyes were the color of dark ink, which gave them a lovely exotic appearance.

The subjugated woman dropped the wheelbarrow and made haste for a bucket. Scott beat her to it. While he handed the full bucket to her, he flashed a wide smile that went all the way up to his gorgeous eyes. Always so kind to her and willing to help, Scott seemed to be looking beyond her eyes to read her intimate thoughts.

No way, it's just my imagination.

When she turned away, Scott noticed a book sticking out of the hip pocket of her jeans. "What are you reading, Margie?"

Her father's gazed snapped in his daughter's direction.

Freezing, Margie's hand slowly made its way to the pocket to feel the curled edges of the book wedged in against her buttock. Her eyes darted like a ping-pong ball from her father to Scott, both of whom were waiting for an answer.

"Margie don't read," Doug said.

Scott's brows furrowed.

Margie tossed the book into the wheelbarrow. "I found it in the shed rows. I was meaning to throw it out. Guess I forgot."

A slice of sunshine burst into the barn when the rickety door creaked open. Mike, Shane, and Coco stepped into the dark dank stable.

The sight of Mike West strolling down the aisle past the horses made Margie's world explode.

God, he's so beautiful. Her dark eyes were transfixed by his strong, square jaw, the way his dark locks brushed across those sexy hazel eyes. There was something complicated in his eyes, something that gave him a mysterious aura. She was so captivated by him that she poured the bucket of water over her father's old battered slippers.

Doug's eyes widened and fury spread across his already churlish pout. "Margie, what the hell's the matter with you?" he shrieked.

She couldn't hear him. She only heard the sound of her heart thrumping in her breast as her Adonis drew closer.

While Mike tried like hell to ignore Margie's glazed-over, puppy love stare boring through him, he couldn't ignore the ornery gleam in his brother's eye, and the devilish curl forming on his lips. He was like Satan himself. He knew what Shane was capable of and prayed that he'd keep it in check.

Margie wasted no time. "Hi, Mike."

"Hey, Margie, how are you?" he asked politely.

"I'm doing just fine, what brings you by?"

The evil chuckle that surged from Shane scraped up Mike's spine and through the top of his head. "He came to see you, Margie."

Mike glowered at his younger brother. A sinister sated smile swept across Shane's ornery face. He was thrilled with the agitation he had wielded in his big brother's direction.

Unanswered prayer. Delighted by the notion, Margie brushed one of the many stray strands of hair behind her ear. "What did you need to see me for, Mike?"

Doug had enough of this foolishness. He slammed the rag into Scott's chest, snatched a pitchfork that was leaning against the wall, and spit brown tobacco juice out the side of his craggy lips before shouldering past Mike to a close-by stall.

"He ain't here to see you, Margie. You weren't never good enough for the likes of him." He tossed a pitchfork full of dirty straw into the wheelbarrow. "Now, what's this about, boys?"

"Coco says you want her horses out of your barn. We've come to take care of that for you." Mike was grateful for the change in topic.

"Well, be my guest, West." He shook the filthy pitchfork at him. "You ain't getting no freaking prize. You'll see." He stabbed the pitchfork into the dirt floor that was inches from Mike's feet. "Get 'em outta here, West, and make it quick."

Scott stepped forward to hand the grey Thoroughbred's lead to Mike and pointed to the stalls where Coco's horses were kept. The Wests each led two horses from the barn. After snapping a lead rope onto the last horse, Doug shoved it at Coco. With a nasty grimace, he made a sharp head gesture toward the barn door. He followed Coco and the horse down the aisle until she came to a stop next to Margie.

She urged a gentle smile at the homely woman. She had tried to make friends with her during her horses' stay at the O'Conner stable, but Doug simply wasn't having it. "Good-bye, Margie."

She stared back at Coco with befuddlement in her lovely dark eyes.

"You have the most beautiful eyes," Coco said.

"Save the bullshit, Beardmore," Doug cursed from behind, "just get that freaking horse outta here."

Coco clucked to the Thoroughbred and continued toward the barn door.

Margie measured her as she walked away. She rather liked her and was always amazed at how pleasant the beauty was. She had always complimented Margie on her eyes, or how pretty her hair could be if she used a certain conditioner or shampoo. Her father was quick to put a stop to such conversations. He didn't have to worry about it anymore.

"Well, Mike's got the blonde, a bundle of training fees, and a whole bunch of trouble," Scott pointed out.

Slamming the barn door, Doug coughed. "Couldn't happen to a better bunch—looking down their long West noses at us." He spewed another stream of brown juice into the floor.

Margie's face wilted and her shoulders slumped.

The barn was no longer bright. The pleasant, pretty woman was no longer a client. Worse, Mike West had made his exit—as he always did. Shrinking onto a bale of straw, she stared at the dirt floor without really seeing it.

"Margie," her foul father roared, "clean them empty stalls."

Slowly, she lifted from the bale. "I gotta dump this load." She pushed the wheelbarrow through the barn door. She hesitated for a moment to watch Mike lead the horses down the shed row, his Levis clinging to his smooth buttocks while he chatted with Coco.

Lord above, how I wish I were Coco Beardmore.

When the group turned the bend and were out of sight, Margie glanced down at the book resting amongst the pile of dung in the wheelbarrow. She snatched the book and wiped what stains she could from the faces of the rapt lovers on the cover. Staring at the words scrolled above their heads, she wished she could read the wonderful story that must lie within the pages.

~ *Two* ~

Among the long white fences of Westwood Thoroughbred Farm, the iridescent droplets of dew clung to the blades of grass. It was as if God had scattered diamonds over night before beckoning His sunbeams to make them glitter to greet the morning.

Eric West slapped the Thoroughbred gelding's rump when he trotted through the gate into the paddock. Smiling, he watched the strong horse snorting, tossing his head, and kicking up his heels in foal-like glee while galloping through the paddock.

Breathing in the fresh day, he raised his face to the wisp of the morning breeze. The mighty oak trees waved their leaves along the winding driveway of the horse farm, and the sunshine glinted off the windows of the Victorian farmhouse that stood on the hill beyond the long, blue roofed barns. His chest always filled with pride when he looked over her, Westwood, the vast Thoroughbred farm he'd raised from ruins. She was now a grand prize he could hand down to generations of Wests.

The rumble of Mike's truck drew his attention past the oaks on the driveway to the stone entrance. Hauling a six-horse Featherlite horse trailer, the silver dually pickup rolled through the archway. Eric's eyes narrowed when he noticed a white Escalade following the truck and trailer. They came to a stop in front of the barn.

Punch and Shane jumped out of the pickup. Mike and a very attractive blonde slid from the seats of the Escalade.

This instantly brought an arch to Eric's eyebrow. The training schedules were tight and they had decided to hold back on accepting new clients for the time being. "What's all this?" he inquired.

"Dad, this is Coco Beardmore, a new customer. We've brought in five horses for her," Mike told him.

Once again admiring a handsome West man, Coco favored him with a smile.

Extremely fit for a man of fifty-five, the patriarch of the West family struck an imposing figure. His dark hair had only a spatter of gray; and, like his sons, he had broad strong shoulders.

Coco offered Eric her hand, which he accepted. "Such a handsome group, you Wests are."

"Beardmore ..." Eric said. "Are you associated with—"

"Her father owns it," Shane interjected.

"Ahhh." Eric shot a look in his older son's direction.

Ducking his father's glance, Mike suggested, "Let's get those horses settled in."

Turning toward the horse trailer, Coco slipped on the loose gravel beneath her and fell to her knees. Racing to help the curvaceous Coco to her feet, Mike and Shane bumped into each other. Mike shot his brother a "back off" look. Scowling, Shane honored his silent, yet lethal, request.

Slightly burned, beads of blood bubbled from the abrasion on her knee. Coco winced.

"Are you okay?" Shane asked.

"I've got her," Mike elbowed him. "You start unloading the horses. I'll take Coco into the barn." After another glowering look, he escorted her toward the door.

No way. Leaving the horses right where they were, Shane followed Mike and the bruised blonde bombshell. "Do you need a band aide, Coco? How about a cool compress?"

Punch rolled his eyes at a baffled Eric.

"I didn't know we were taking on new customers." Eric folded his arms over his chest while taking in his sons' *Three Stooges* act.

"Well, most of our customers don't look like that," Punch said. "I guess I'm unloading the horses." He strolled to the back of the horse trailer.

Kate West wandered out of the barn at the same time her brothers were stumbling in while hovering over the limping lovely. Considering the fuss that was taking place, she held the door open for them. "Who's the sex kitten?" she asked her father.

"Her name's Coco."

"What's she doing here?"

Glancing at his sons, he shrugged his shoulder. "I'm not sure." Deciding it was a good idea to change the subject, Eric nodded toward her car. "When are you picking up your new car?"

Her mood brightened. "In a day or two."

He glanced at her three-year-old sage Altima parked in the driveway. The sun gleamed off its chrome. It didn't have a scratch on it. "Your old car isn't in bad condition."

Kate wrinkled her nose. "I know. But that's just a car."

CB 80 CR 80

The evening draped its dark purple light over Westwood Farm. Kate massaged her hair in a towel before letting the blonde ringlets spill out across her damp shoulders. Droplets of water trickled down her spine when she pulled a soft cami over her torso and slipped into a comfy pair of pajama pants.

Her days were long. In the morning, she was an assistant to the track veterinarian. Dr. Ben Spears was a crotchety old man, and that was one of his most endearing virtues. After arriving home around noon, she would make her rounds through the farm's stables to rub down this horse or slap a white thick poultice on the legs of another.

Ahhh, the day is over. It's time to relax, and make the final decision on that hot Mustang.

She lay across her bed.

A gentle breeze inflated the curtains into fat billows, and then sucked them back against the screen. The tiny flame of the candle on her vanity flickered in the waft to blow the scent of honeysuckle through the room.

Ready to examine the features available on the brand-spanking-new Mustangs, she opened her laptop. With a tap of her fingertip, the sporty convertible's color would change from blazing red to a rich silver to a shiny ebony.

Hmmm, the red is really sexy.

Leaning back against her pillows, she bit her lip and became completely lost in concentration while trying to picture herself in the sweet little ride. Her dream of whizzing along the highway with her blonde mane whipping in the wind was broken by the sound of a loud snort and a rustle of the shrubs below her bedroom window.

Looking up from the laptop, Kate's eyes narrowed. She listened intently. Nothing. Shrugging her shoulder, she returned her attention to the Ford dealership's website. The colors of the glorious Mustangs changed. Red. Silver. Black.

03 80 03 80

The study was dimly lit. The glow of the computer screen on Eric's desk cast a soft, blue hue over the handsome man's face while he studied race results on the Churchill Downs web page. He slipped his glasses from his face and rubbed his eyes.

Munching on a sandwich, Shane wandered into the room, plunked down on the sofa, and propped his feet on the coffee table before taking another big bite.

Rapping his fingers on the desk, Eric stared at the youngest West with his lips pursed until the sandy-haired man looked up. Eric pointed sharply at his feet.

Clearing his throat, Shane jerked them from the coffee table. "Tom Mason is supposed to call me sometime tomorrow afternoon."

His father chuckled. "Tom is a very old friend of mine, but don't forget that he's new to the Thoroughbred game. He wants to talk about a swimming program for his horse, but he's not exactly convinced that horses should be swimming. He's worried the horse will sink."

"Don't worry, Dad. I can be very persuasive when I wanna be."

"When he calls, talk slowly."

"Wait a minute, isn't this the guy that you're always getting wedding invitations from?" Shane asked.

The thought of his eccentric friend prompted another chuckle. "Oh yeah, Tom's been married and married. His wives seem to be getting younger and younger. I think his last wife was twelve."

"They say there's someone for everyone," Shane said. "How old is he anyway?"

"Fifty-one. Maybe fifty-two. Tom's charming in a very clumsy sort of way. His fourth—Or was it his third wedding? Anyway, Tom and his newest bride were having their first dance together—" Eric snorted while trying to suppress his amusement. "He stepped on her gown and ripped the entire skirt off." He burst into chuckles. "I shouldn't laugh. It really was terrible. But there she stood with a blue garter around her thigh while wearing a white thong. That marriage lasted only a year."

He and Shane laughed.

"Yeah, Tom is very well-to-do," Eric said. "He doesn't have any trouble finding someone."

ଔ   ଅ   ଔ   ଅ

Kate found herself ambivalent between the blazing red Mustang and the classic ebony sports car. Both were convertibles, and both were hot. She couldn't make a decision. Unconsciously, she nibbled at her pinky fingernail. The sound of a horse whinnying broke her deliberation. The whinny was followed by hooves shuffling through grass. Then, there was a loud squeal.

She set the laptop aside and tip-toed to the window. The silhouette of a grey horse trotting through the yard like a phantom in the moonlight caught her eye. While straining to see where he had gone, she spied five more. Kicking and nipping at each other, the group of escapees were galloping up and down the driveway.

"Cripes." Grumbling, she slipped on a pair of flip-flops and dashed from her bedroom. Her shoes *thump, thump, thumped* against her feet while she hurried down the sweeping staircase, past the grandfather's clock in the foyer, and into the study.

"Dad! Shane! Loose horses!"

Shane and Eric rushed to the bay window and pinched back the curtains.

"How did they get out?" Shane asked.

"It doesn't much matter," Eric said. "Let's go."

03 80 03 80

Mike had decided to retire early. After taking a hot shower, he pulled on a comfortable pair of lounging pants, and grabbed a Yuengling beer from the fridge. He sank into the sofa in front of the stone fireplace that climbed to the open beams of his bungalow on the far side of Westwood Farm.

He and his wife, Ava, used to live in the charming bungalow together, but their marriage had ended after five years. At the age of thirty-three, he was a bachelor once again

He plunked his legs on the coffee table. Crossed his left ankle over his right, and clicked on the fifty-two-inch flat-screen TV mounted over the mantle.

Droplets of moisture drizzled down the brown beer bottle, dangled, and then trickled onto his bare chiseled chest. Click after click of the remote, sip after sip of the chilled beer, he failed to find anything worth watching.

"A million channels, and there's never anything good on." He turned the TV off and pitched the remote onto the coffee table.

It was quiet evenings like this, with shit for TV, that Ava crept into his thoughts. He couldn't help himself. The loneliness getting the better of him would catapult him down a sultry memory lane. He was always amazed how strong his weakness for her was. Oh yeah, the way her auburn hair swept across the pillows. The sheets would lie lightly over her breasts. The way they lifted and fell with each breath with her hard nipples pushing like petite pebbles through the silken sheets. The way her full plump lips pressed against his.

God, she was hot.

When he found himself lost in thoughts of Ava, he mostly thought about her mesmerizing green eyes—the great manipulators. When she looked at him with those, he was a goner. She could pluck out his very soul.

Unfortunately, she plucked at lots of men's souls. Yep, that's right. Ava was a cheater—a big one.

He shook his head in disgust with her, but more with himself. He took another swig of the smooth beer. *C'mon Mike, it's time to forgive and forget. Time to forgive yourself for being so damned stupid, and try like hell to forget she ever existed.* But that was the proverbial "easier said than done" routine.

He bumped into Ava on a regular basis at the racetrack. She worked for Dr. Spears on the days Kate didn't. If Kate worked the morning shift with Spears, Ava would work the evening.

Although they were cordial toward one and other, there was always tension between them. It was sexual tension—on Mike's part anyway. She still held a fistful of his soul. He hated it, but try as he might, he couldn't escape it.

Forgetting that Ava existed was not very viable. Well, maybe not. Mike scrubbed his fingers across the evening bristle on his chin, and took another long cool swig of Yuengling. *Hmmm, Coco may be the fix I need to clear my head of Ava. Hey, I can picture that. Now there's a viable option. Sure, she seems a bit clumsy, but she might move like a freaking ballerina in the sack.*

With the beer bottle resting on his chest, he laid his head back against the sofa. He closed his eyes. The corners of his mouth turned upward. *Ya know, that ballerina scenario ain't half bad.* The erotic images he was allowing his mind to conjure was severed by the sound of hooves stomping through gravel and familiar voices hollering from outside.

Mike jumped from the sofa, the beer bottle sweat skittered down his chest into his navel. Dabbing at the dribble on his chest, he peered out the front window in time to see Coco's grey gelding gallop through his front yard with Kate in pursuit. He pulled on his boots to join the chase.

CB EO CR EO

Forty-five minutes later; Eric, Kate, Shane, and Mike wearily led the five horses through the barn door. Eric flipped on the barn lights. Their eyes widened, and their mouths dropped open. Mike groaned.

Straw and hay was strewn about the aisle. Stall doors hung lop-sided from their mountings. Rakes, buckets, and pitchforks were tossed over the floor; and wheelbarrows were overturned. Several horses wandered through the barn and munched on the broken bales of hay.

"What a mess," Kate said. "These guys have been loose for a while."

"I wonder who the escape artist is," Shane said.

"Something tells me it's Charlatan." Mike shot the horse a dirty look. It almost seemed that the horse shrugged at him with indifference.

Tired, hot, and sweaty, Eric glared at Mike with flared nostrils.

Managing to avoid his father's gaze, Mike guided the grey gelding into a stall.

Holding tight to his glare, Eric picked up a rake and shoved it into Mike's chest. Then, he marched out the barn door with Kate and Shane behind him.

Staring at the mess, Mike leaned against the rake while the loose horses enjoyed their extra portions of hay. He groaned and glanced back at Charlatan, who snorted at him through the bars of his stall.

~ *Three* ~

The morning sun splashed across Westwood Thoroughbred Farm. The business of Thoroughbreds was well under way.

Scuttling around the barn, the stable hands pushed wheelbarrows heaped with steaming horse manure, filled buckets with fresh water, and led horses from once place to another. Their Spanish chatter almost drowned-out Taylor Swift's voice, which filtered in through the barn radio. A deafening *bang, bang, bang*, reverberated down the aisle every once in a while.

Rubbing his eyes and yawning, Mike slid through the barn door. The *Bang, bang, bang*, caught his attention, but when he looked up, he saw Coco propped against the wall halfway down the aisle. The annoying noise was all but forgotten when he saw Shane leaning over her. Mike had seen that stance before. Speaking in a low cool voice, he was entertaining her with his oh-so-charming Shane smile while trying to woo Coco into a romantic rendezvous.

The left side of Mike's mouth sucked in, and his eyes fell into chary slits. *Hmmmm.* A young Mexican stable hand wandered past with an empty wheelbarrow—well, almost empty. A mushy green piece of horse dung clung to the corner. *Perfect.* His eyes brighten while the left side of his lip turned upward.

"Perdone, por favor." *Excuse me, please.* Swiping the wheelbarrow, Mike pushed it down the aisle at a jog while aiming from his brother's backside.

Casting him a coquettish smile, Coco relaxed against the wall to allow Shane to charm her. She was rather enjoying it. By her calculations, he was at least seven years her junior. *He sure is cute. Shamefully handsome, and they tended to be so much fun at that age.*

Bang, bang, bang! The horse's hooves continued to smack the stall wall.

Shane was in full seduction mode. "I was thinking a picnic by the lake this evening would be really nice." He looked into her blue eyes, down her throat, and—hell yeah—to the ample cleavage the woman couldn't help but flaunt.

Suddenly, his legs were knocked out from underneath him. Slamming into the bucket of the wheelbarrow, his body jerked backward. Mike's ornery grin beamed down at him. He could feel the wetness of a warm slimy substance seeping through his jeans. No one had to tell him, he recognized that smell. He scowled at his older brother. *Okay, let the pissing match begin.*

Cupping her hands over her mouth, Coco stepped back.

Bang, bang, bang! The hooves seemed like they were breaking through the kickboards.

Agitation etched across his face, Punch stepped out of the stall with sweat on his brow. He peered down at Shane's scarlet face. Mike stood back with a *take-that-asshole* sneer while his brother eased his way out of the wheelbarrow.

"I'm glad you guys are having such a good time. I could use a hand in here." The frustration crept into Punch's voice. Mike and Coco followed him into the stall. Trying to wipe the soggy green crap from his butt, Shane shuffled along behind.

Charlatan's eyes were like saucers. His ears were pinned flat to his head, and his nostrils were flared. Tossing his head, he jabbed sharply with his hoof against the wall. *Bang!*

Dodging the kick, the Mexican exercise rider landed on top of the tiny exercise saddle laying up-side-down in the corner. Beads of sweat dotting his dark complexion, he glanced back at the obnoxious grey gelding.. He scrambled to his feet, slid along the wall, and skedaddled out the door.

Punch grabbed the gelding's lead rope. "He's a real jackass. I've been trying to saddle him for twenty minutes."

The horse snorted and yanked back on the lead, he reared and punched out with his front hooves.

Punch jerked down on the lead. "Easy now."

"You're being too rough with him," Coco said. "Charlatan just needs some love and understanding. That's all."

"I was thinking more like a two-by-four." Mike watched the snarling Charlatan stomp and pull back from Punch's hold.

"Michael West ..."

Mike reached up and grabbed the gelding's ear. He twisted it in his fist. Dragging Punch across the stall, Charlatan pitched his head wildly until he forced Mike to let go.

Taking it all in from a distance, Shane leaned against the threshold of the stall. He scratched his head. "You want the twitch?"

"Yeah," Mike yelled back while trying to help Punch gain control.

Shane turned to retrieve the heavy handled device with a loop of thick rope attached to the top. They would have to slip the horse's upper lip through the rope, and then twist until it was taut around the lip, which caused great discomfort until it forced him to settle down and submit.

Filled with disdain, Coco gasped and grabbed Shane by his sleeve. "No, I don't like twitches. They're inhumane."

Shane grew a cock-eyed smirk while once again catching a glimpse of her full cleavage. "Yeah, Mike, they're kinda inhumane."

The horse whirled his hind quarters around while taking a quick jab at Punch who stepped out of the way. "You want a shot at this, boy?" he asked Shane.

The horse yanked away from their grip. Tossing his head, he reared high into the air and danced on his hind feet, until he toppled over backward. Mike and Punch jumped back while the horse struggled to organize his feet before finally leaping up.

"He's a flipper," Mike said. "When he becomes agitated, he throws himself backward. Coco, how many time has this horse flipped?"

Gnawing on her manicured pinky, Coco demurred, "Well, ah, maybe once or twice."

Mike's suspicious gaze overwhelmed her.

"Okay, quite a few times, but only when provoked."

Punch blinked hard. "Provoked? You mean like being saddled?" When Coco lifted a shoulder at him, he realized why Doug was so willing to give the horses up without much of a fuss. What were the other four horses capable of doing? His shock shifted to irritation.

Coco grabbed a bag of peppermints from her purse. Charlatan's ears stood straight up at the sound of rustling paper. His eyes wide, he snorted when she stretched out her hand toward him with the plump round peppermint in her palm. The horse snatched the candy and sucked on it like a baby sucking on a pacifier. Stroking his thick muscled neck, she whispered, "There now, isn't that better?"

With a searing stare, Punch turned to Mike. "You've got to be kidding me, dude."

After a short deliberation, Mike and Punch decided to give Charlatan a shower and shelf the morning gallop until they could devise a plan. This seemed to be the best idea since the exercise rider was nowhere to be found.

While he turned his attention to one of Coco's more cooperative Thoroughbreds, Mike suggested Punch move on to other horses.

03   80   03   80

The equine swimming facility was located at the far end of the stables. The Wests had added it three years earlier in order to provide a low-impact way to exercise horses to build better lung capacity and strong lean muscle without constantly pounding on their joints.

The afternoon sun beamed through the tall arched windows lining the perimeter of the facility to glint off the water in the pool. A long ramp dropped into the water for the horse to enter the swimming area and the walls were curved inward so that it could not climb out.

Mike and Coco could hear the soft hum of the pump when they went inside.

The strong smell of chlorine wafted through the facility where, from the edge, Shane was guiding a horse, snorting with every stroke of his legs, around the pool with a long staff attached to its halter. The horse's ears were perked, his nostrils flared, and his head bopped up and down above the water while he swam.

Mike led a sleek sorrel mare that seemed harmless enough into the shower stall on the far end of the facility. "We have to give her a shower before she can swim," he explained to Coco. "That way the pool stays clean."

Nodding her head, Coco grabbed the hose from the hook on the wall and sprayed Mike hard in the chest when she depressed the nozzle. Her eyes widened and her mouth dropped. She grabbed her mouth with her hand. It seemed that Coco wass full of no-no's. Some were easier to deal with than others.

Forcing a smile, Mike decided that every time the beautiful bombshell pulled a no-no, he would picture her naked. While the water soaked into his shirt to suck it against his chiseled chest, he made this one of those moments.

"I'm sorry," she said through her fingers.

He removed the nozzle from her hand. "I'll take it from here," he replied with a calm that was as forced as his smile.

Across the pool, Shane's cell phone played the tune *Brown Sugar* from The Rolling Stones.

"Hello. … Oh, Mr. Mason, I've been expecting your call," he said into the phone while guiding the snorting horse through the water.

Coco nuzzled and cooed at the mare while Mike finished her shower. "Shane should almost be finished with that one." He called out across the pool, "Are you almost done?"

Nodding to him, Shane continued his conversation with Tom Mason.

Coco watched Shane lead the horse through the water. Just walking around the pool while holding the guide staff seemed simple enough. "That looks like fun," she said. "Can I try to swim mine, Mikey?" With a coquettish smile, she batted her long lashes.

"It's Mike."

He wasn't at all sure that Coco was up to the task. The last thing he needed today was to have to fish her out of the pool. On the other hand, it really wasn't that difficult to do. On the other hand, if she fell in, she could get hurt. On the other hand, that tight shirt she was wearing would show-off a lot of stuff if it were soaked. He was all out of hands while picturing her naked. The two things weren't jiving.

"I'll tell you what … I'll get her started, and then you can take over for a few minutes."

Okay. That seems like a safe arrangement. I'll be right there with her in case she pulls a no-no, like tripping over herself and taking a flying leap into the semi-clean horse water.

Mike led the mare toward the ramp when he spied an extra guide staff at the other end of the pool. "Can you get that staff for me, Coco?"

"Sure." Delighted to help, she trotted toward the staff and past Shane.

Not at all concerned with Coco's movements, Shane continued to talk on his cell phone while guiding the horse toward the ramp. "I assure you, Mr. Mason, this is the safest form of training you can do. For the horse as well as the person …" he pledged, just as Coco bent over to pick up the long staff.

Mike's gaze fell upon her smoothly curved derrière. Instantly, alarms went off in his head that she would strike Shane with the staff and knock him into the water. Panicked, Mike dropped the horse's lead. He dashed toward Coco, snatched the staff from her grip, swung it around, and cracked Shane in the back.

His eyes wide, Shane teetered at the rim of the pool with his arms flailing in circles. Coco's gasp at Mike's sudden action distracted him, which caused him to swing the staff in the opposite direction and smack his brother in the stomach.

"Wh-wh-whoa!" Shane plunged head-first into the water.

Frantic, the Thoroughbred trounced in the pool. Shane surfaced to face the horse's hooves thrashing through the water toward him. He needed to steer clear or be severely cut. Trying to push away from the animal, he swooshed his hands backward. The horse grunted at the chlorine now splashing into his eyes. His panic piqued.

Coco grabbed the staff. "Shane, get hold," she called to him.

Shane swam toward the edge. Bouncing off the side of the pool, the staff poked the horse in the face to agitate it more, which created more thrashing. While dodging the horse's hooves, Shane pawed at the water until he clutched the staff and managed to lift it over his head.

Coco leaned over the edge of the pool. The wet, slick, wooden staff slipped through Shane's hands several times before she finally grabbed hold of it.

"Whoa, easy now," Coco whispered to the animal while gingerly guiding it toward the ramp.

Mike managed to hoist Shane, huffing and puffing, from the pool. In a puddle of chlorine water, he collapsed onto the cement floor. Much to his own surprise, he found the cell phone still in his hand. Gulping for air and blinking his eyes from the nip of the chlorine, he lifted the phone to his face.

"Mr. Mason ... Mr. Mason?" No reply. "Great. Hey thanks, bro." Grumbling, he pitched the phone into the pool.

Mike's face flushed.

CB ED CR ED

Enough is enough for one day, Mike thought.

It seemed like a wise decision to not bother with any more of Coco's horses for the rest of the day. After gathering Shane up from the wet cement, they put the two Thoroughbreds away. Having been on the receiving end of dirty looks from Punch earlier, and now Shane wielding the same expressions in his direction, Mike considered it a brilliant decision to send Coco home. She looped her arm through Mike's when he escorted her to the barn door. He wondered if she was picturing him naked after his poor judgment call at the pool.

"I'd love you to come for dinner at my house tonight, Mike," she said. "I know it's probably hard to believe, but I'm actually a very good cook."

In fact, yes, it was very hard for him to believe, but he was so busy with the birthday suit thing, that he found himself most agreeable. "I'm sure you are."

Biting her lip, she gently stroked his wet chest while churning out in a soft, sensual tone. "Are you sure Shane will be all right?"

He didn't care what happened. Even though it was his no-no and not hers, he was picturing those full, firm, fantastic breasts. *Shane? Shane who?* Mike blinked back into the moment. "Oh, yeah, he'll be fine. It was just an unscheduled bath, that's all."

She giggled like a schoolgirl. "Do you think Mr. Mason will swim his horses?"

"We'll see." He opened the door of her SUV.

She stroked his cheek before she slipped into the driver's seat. Then, she drew his face close and kissed his lips while caressing them with her tongue. When she pulled away she thought that he would look damn good naked.

"See you tonight around seven," she said while starting the vehicle and shoving it into reverse.

Slowly, the SUV backed.

Catching a glimpse of Shane walking past with his dripping shirt over his arm, Coco's eyes veered from the rear-view mirror. Her eyes fixated on his wet sculpted pecks. His tight abs glistened in the sunshine.

The SUV backed.

She licked her lips when he stopped to wring out his shirt in the driveway.

The SUV backed.

Droplets of water dripped down Shane's broad shoulders, biceps, and over his tight belly while the water poured from the shirt.

The SUV backed.

"Coco, watch out." Mike's voice ripped through her diversion.

Her attention jolted back to the driveway at the very moment the Escalade sideswiped Mike's six-horse trailer. The sound of metal ripping and curling reverberated through the farm. Horrified, Coco slammed on the brakes.

Shane stopped wringing-out his shirt.

Kate and Punch rushed from the barn.

Mike darted toward the Escalade.

Their faces fell in shock at the sight of the smashed trailer that was tangled up with the SUV.

Mike yanked open her door. "Are you all right? What were you doing?"

Dry, her mouth moved but nothing came out for a few seconds. "I don't know. I'm so sorry," she wailed.

Kate leaned in close to Shane. "She is so not for him."

Shane sighed. "Wait till he checks out the damage."

Pursing his lips, Punch expelled a long downward whistle that was accompanied by a wince.

Afraid to look, Mike approached the trailer and cringed. Squeezing his eyes closed, he tried to remain cool.

Naked ... She's gorgeous naked. Try like hell to picture her.

Naked.

Naked ballerina.

Okay, just naked.

He opened his eyes. "Coco, pull forward ... very slowly." His voice was tight.

Smothering whimpers, Coco bit her lip. Shoving the Escalade into DRIVE, she pressed the accelerator gently. The tinny echoes of ripping metal skittered up Mike's stiffened spine. It seemed like forever. Finally, there was a loud pop, and the two vehicles were separated.

Gasping, Coco jumped from her SUV and clutched her mouth with her hand. "I'm so sorry," she said repeatedly with great remorse.

Mike took in a deep, frustrated breath. His brain was betraying him. Try as he might, he couldn't imagine the buxom blonde beauty naked. He needed her to leave immediately. "I'll see you later. ...Okay?"

Coco cowered. "Okay, Mike. I'll see you at seven." She stopped to measure the damages to her white Escalade. While bending over to run her hand over the curled, smashed bumper; her shirt hiked up enough to reveal a butterfly tattoo that swept daintily across her lower back.

Kate's eyes brightened. She jabbed Shane with her elbow. "Nice tramp stamp."

Shane's face lit-up. He leaned into Punch. "A little bit of ba-donk-a-freakin'-donk going on."

"Mmmm, mmm, mmm," was all Punch could manage.

They watched Coco drive up the driveway, past the grand oaks, and through the stone entrance.

Pallid, Mike dragged his fingers through his dark hair and cupped his hand on the nape of his neck while staring at his trashed trailer. "I'm going to the track."

"What for?" Punch asked.

"To get some information on Coco's horses."

"Who ya gonna talk to?" Shane wanted to know.

"Someone who'll tell me anything I want to know. Margie O'Conner." He went to his truck.

"You might have to put out," Shane joked. When Punch chuckled along, he continued, "Take one for the team."

"Not even with a ten-foot pole, buddy," Mike assured the two laughing hyenas.

~ *Four* ~

Sitting on a bale of hay, Margie O'Conner wiped down a bridle with an old filthy rag. Next to the bale, a pile of bridles waited their turn for her to clean them. She examined the leather on the bridle and the bit to make sure it was spotless. *Perfect.* She set the bridle aside and picked up the next in line.

Doug always kept her busy with cleaning stalls, hauling water, and grooming the horses. When she wasn't at the track, she was doing laundry or cleaning the shack-of-a-house they lived in at the far end of Lanzville.

When a strand of her mousey brown hair fell loose from the rubber band to tickle her nose, she combed the mop with her fingers to tidy up her ponytail. An old Charlie Rich song filtered through the radio. Unlike the other stables along the shed rows, the radio was never tuned to the popular country western music stations. As far as her father was concerned; Johnny Cash, Loretta Lynn, and Waylon Jennings—those were the *real* country western singers. She didn't dare touch the dial on the old battered radio—Doug would have a stroke.

In looking for something else to occupy her mind while she scrubbed green horse salvia from a bit, Margie noticed something resting on top of an over-turned bucket. She put down the bridle to investigate.

It was a book.

She remembered seeing Scott reading it earlier in the day. He looked so content with his glasses parked on his nose while submerged in the story. She fingered the words on the sleek cover.

Earlier, when she had asked him what he was reading, he said, "It's a book about a solider in the Civil War. I like historical books. What kind of books do you like?" There he was again—looking into her eyes while waiting for a response as if her opinion mattered.

Margie was most taken aback by the question and the way his beautiful compassionate eyes always probed hers. Dropping her gaze, she searched her mind. Unbeknownst to her father, some of her mother's old paperbacks were still in a box in the corner of the basement.

"I like the ones with the good-looking guys holding the pretty girls on the front," she blurted out.

Scott's eyes fell into a squint. "Do you mean romance-type books?"

"Ummm, yep, those are the ones," she lied. "You seem pretty smart, Scott. What are you still doing here? Why didn't you go on to college instead of mucking stalls and living in the trailer park?"

He studied her for a moment before lifting a shoulder. "Mom didn't have the money to send me to school. No one from our family ever went to college. Everyone worked here at the track at one time or another. Then when mom got sick—Well, I had to stick around. It's okay. It all worked out." He returned to his book.

She felt bad for him. He was stuck with Keystone Downs—the same way she was.

She picked up the left-behind book and perused the pages. Her eyes narrowed. She recognized a word here or there. Easy words like: *to, the, and, it,* and *horse.* She knew that word well, that was a word that was on almost every sign around the racetrack, *"horse".* But the rest she couldn't decipher. Wishing she could, she shrugged. She replaced the book on the bucket and shuffled back to the bale of straw, and pile of dirty bridles.

Charlie Rich crooned, *"Behind closed doors..."* Sighing, she submitted to hum along as if she had a choice in the matter.

The early evening sunshine sliced into the barn when the door creaked open. The backwash of bright light provided only the silhouette of a man standing in the threshold. His broad shoulders eased down through his slender hips. "Hey, Margie, what's going on?" Mike West's voice carried like a song down the aisle.

Her face lit-up. She pitched the rag to the floor, brushed back a frock of hair from her eyes, and wiped her hands on her cruddy jeans. "Hi, Mike. What brings you by?" She tried to smother a nervous giggle.

"Coco's horses." He walked down the aisle to perch his boot on the bale next to her.

Margie's face drooped. Her shoulders slumped. She snatched up the rag and returned to her chore. *Coco Beardmore, no freaking kidding.* "My father ain't here, and I don't know when he'll be back," she said with a cool, clipped tone.

"I was hoping you could help me," he said with an easy smile.

Stopping in mid-chore, she peered at him askance. "With what?"

"How smart is that big grey gelding, Charlatan?"

Margie sighed. After contemplating Mike's question, and his gorgeous, piercing hazel eyes for a moment; she tossed the rag to the floor with a disgusted groan.

Oh, it isn't him. It's me, and the fact that I can't help myself. True, Mike West would never give me the time of day unless he needed something. Why should he? Look at him, just look at him, he's fabulous. What's wrong with Ava West? Carrying on with other men the way she does. If I had Mike, I'd never look at another man.

She stood up. "C'mon, I'll show you."

Following her toward the stable office, he glanced down with surprise at her attractive figure. She was slender and tall. Her ripped jeans resembled the designer label called *hard freaking work*, but they clung to her tight shapely buttocks. He noticed the startling gentle sway of her hips when she walked.

She stopped abruptly at the office door and turned to him. Suddenly nose-to-nose with unattractive end of Margie O'Conner, he jumped back, which sent him tumbling over a bale of hay. He landed sprawled on his back into the dirt.

"Coco rubbing off on you?" Chuckling, she held out her rugged man-hand, but he managed to scramble to his feet without touching her. She opened the door to the office and invited him inside with a chilled nod.

Doug O'Conner's office was pretty much a reflection of its owner: old and crusty. The walls were paneled with dirty rough-cut lumber. Faded win pictures hung crooked on the walls among weathered bridles and dirty clipboards. A beat-up desk littered with tattered race programs, ashtrays filled to the brim with crushed half-smoked cigarette butts, filthy coffee mugs, and several empty cans of Copenhagen filled one corner. A brick substituting for one of the legs was stuffed under a corner of the desk.

Covered with a thick layer of dust, a small black-and-white TV and an old VCR rested on a rickety stand next to the desk. Margie gestured to a scarred wooden chair near it, but Mike politely declined with a wave of his hand.

She pushed the door closed with a loud clap. Uncomfortable with being in a small, closed-in room with her, Mike flinched. The anxiety etched on his face did not go unnoticed, but she let him off the hook and got to the business at hand.

"Every morning we'd come into a wrecked barn," she said, "Charlatan and his friends would really work the place over every night." She slipped a battered tape into the VCR. "Dad got sick of it, so we set-up a close-circuit TV to see who the smarty-pants in the group was. Watch this." She poked a screw driver into a hole where the power button used to be and turned it, the screen lit up to a dull gray.

A wobbly image of the barn aisle filled the screen. Gradually, a stall door jerked, bumped, and then slid open. Charlatan stepped out of his stall and meandered down the aisle while plucking mouthfuls of hay from the bales stacked along the walls.

Stopping at a stall, he nuzzled the horse through the bars. Then, with proficiency, he unlatched the stall door with his teeth, and slid it open. Repeating the routine, he continued down the aisle until five horses wandered freely through the barn to munch on the stacked bales and knock over pitchforks, wheelbarrows, and buckets of water.

"Well, I'll be damned. We've got a regular Houdini on our hands." Mike was most impressed.

"He's very smart," she said. "Funny how he only lets out some of the horses. His buddies, I guess."

"We'll fix that."

"Good luck."

Mike turned from the TV. She was so close to him that her breath feathered his face. He swiftly eased away. "Well, thanks for the information, Margie."

"Sure." She looked into those mysterious hazel eyes. *He's uncomfortable, but maybe if he got to know me better, that would change.* She wanted it so badly to change that she decided to take a leap. "Hey, Mike, I'm making my famous fried chicken for supper. Dad will be at the bar for a while. You wanna come over?"

Now Mike's body language was shrieking. His eyes immediately darted to the closed door. Struggling, he stammered for words. "Oh … I'd love to, Margie …" *What luck!* He remembered his other engagement. "I'm having dinner with Coco tonight. Maybe some other time."

By the look on Margie's face, he knew the words didn't come out well. They sure as hell didn't go over big.

She bit her lip and dropped her gaze to the floor. Abruptly, she lifted her chin, marched to the door, and yanked it open. "Sure."

"Thanks again, Margie." He scooted out the door as fast as he could.

She slammed the door behind him and leaned against it. Her breath boomed inside her head and chest. Much to her own surprise, she wasn't feeling helplessly contrite like she usually did when she saw him in the shed rows, and he didn't acknowledge her. After all, it was no secret—not even to her—that she was no raving beauty.

No, she was feeling rather unabashed and resentful. Hot tears welled in her eyes. *Maybe Ava isn't so crazy. Cocky, that's what he is. Maybe Ava gave him just what he deserved. I'd like to give him what he deserves. Not really, I'd like to give him anything he wants.*

Those very thoughts angered her more than Mike's rejection.

She ripped the rubber band that held her ponytail out of her hair. Her long locks tumbled wildly over her shoulders when she raked her harried hands through it. One furious kick sent the rickety chair toppling over. She grabbed several of the empty Copenhagen cans and hurled them at the small TV. With a swipe of one arm, she sent the race programs flying from the desk to scatter over the floor.

She stopped and buried her face in her hands. *Men like Mike West only look at beautiful women. How do they put it? "Beauty is only skin deep, but ugly is to the bone." Is that how he sees me? Bone ugly?*

Needing to calm down, she picked up the chair and plopped down in it. A long sigh escaped her and she wiped the tears from her flushed cheeks.

It is what it is, she ruefully decided.

Cʒ ᴤʌ Cʀ ᴤʌ

Mike hurried from the O'Conner stable. He wanted to get as much distance between him and Margie's dinner invitation as possible.

He was concerned that there may be a small calculated risk in having dinner at Coco's place with her preparing the dinner—on a stove.

Actually, he was feeling bad. He had hurt Margie's feelings. *C'mon. She didn't really think I wanted to have dinner with her. Not that she isn't a perfectly nice person. She just isn't my type. I'm not sure whose type she would be.*

Mike's guilt-trip was interrupted when he bumped into Scott and sent the poor guy to the pavement. He whipped his hand out to help him up. "Sorry, man, I didn't see you."

"No problem." Scott was jovial as always. "What're you doing here?"

"I came by to see Margie."

Scott's voice sounded stiff. "Margie?"

Mike found the change in his tone and the look in his eyes surprising. It was the look of suspicion and jealousy. *How weird is that?* "Yeah, again, sorry I knocked you over." He clapped his hand on Scott's shoulder while trying to smooth any ruffled feathers before hurrying on his way.

Shell-shocked, Scott stared while Mike disappeared around the corner. *Why would Mike West ever want to spend five minutes with Margie?* He pressed through the barn door at the same time she stepped out of the office. His eyes grew to the size of dinner plates at the sight of her adjusting her flannel shirt. Her hair was askew, her cheeks were flushed, and she wore a resolute expression in her eyes.

She stopped when she noticed him. "Scott, what're you doing here?"

He stared at her for a moment before blinking hard. "I forgot my book." He reached for the paperback on the bucket.

"Oh." She hummed along with Tammy Wynette on the radio, "*Stand by your man ...*" while strolling down the aisle.

~ *Five* ~

Tilting back his head, the golden Cocker Spaniel let out a growl mixed with a whine while wagging his tail in an effort to capture Coco's attention.

It was all for not.

She was much too busy caressing her plump lips with a pink blush lipstick. She sat back in the zebra-striped chair to admire her handiwork in the vanity mirror. Her blonde hair cascaded around her downy shoulders, and her supple breasts lifted from the black satin and lace bra.

The three-caret diamond stud earrings that her ex-husband, Henry, had given her for her thirtieth birthday winked at her from the open jewel box. She picked them up and dipped them into her earlobes. They glimmered in the soft glow of her bedroom.

Every time she wore the earrings she would think of her ex.

Henry Snodgrass was an investment counselor to some of the world's most influential and wealthy people. Almost twenty-five years Coco's senior, he had been widowed only four months when her father had introduced them at a Beardmore Industries' Christmas cocktail party.

It was Henry who had opened up the world of Thoroughbred racing for her. He taught her how to read a racing form, handicap the ponies, and make an "educated" choice, or at least a good guess. That was four years ago.

With a sigh, she stood up and admired the lacey, black g-string she had purchased that afternoon.

Perfect.

When the doorbell rang, the Cocker Spaniel jumped to his feet and scampered down the stairs while barking like a Rottweiler. Quickly, Coco slipped into the saucy little black dress she had also purchased to go with the satin and lace bra, and the g-string. Creating cleavage sure to make Mike salivate, the little black dress clung to all the right places.

Perfect.

CB EO CR EO

While waiting on the steps of Coco's brownstone townhouse, Mike hoped his evening would be worth the trashed trailer and, anticipated, acute case of heartburn. He cocked his head when he heard what sounded like a large dog growling and barking from behind the lavishly beveled front door. He looked around at the townhouses with sporty Mercedes, Porsches, and BMW's parked in their driveways before glancing over his shoulder at his pickup parked next to Coco's wrecked SUV.

When the door finally opened the Cocker Spaniel sprung out to circle his legs while sniffing, barking, and snarling at him.

"Booger, behave." Coco looked like forgiveness wrapped in a little black peel-me-off dress when she appeared in the doorway. "Don't worry, he doesn't bite. Come in, Mike," she said like a spider coaxing a fly.

She guided him through the foyer into a living room decked-to-the-hilt with stylish, French provincial furnishings. Following close behind, Booger sniffed and nipped at Mike's legs.

Beautiful paintings hung on the walls in ornate frames. Mike knew exactly one thing about artwork: Jackshit. But it was obvious, even to him, that these pieces had come from a gallery, rather than a retail store. The vibrant colors splashed across the canvas were thick, and sweeping, and perhaps a little angry, that much he could appreciate—kinda.

A gilded mirror hung on the wall behind the sofa. Crystal framed photographs of Coco and her father filled the coffee tables. *Classy.*

"Make yourself comfortable. I'll be right back." She slipped through the doorway into the kitchen.

Mike buried his hands into the pockets of his Levis and studied an abstract work of art on the wall. *What the hell is that supposed to be?*

Booger's growl thinned to a low grouse. His curly ears perked, and he stomped his paws against the white carpet.

"What's the matter, boy?" Purring cautiously at the spunky spaniel, he patted Booger on the head, and then turned his attention to a photo of Stanley Beardmore with his arms wrapped around Coco. Booger sprung at him and clamped his little body around Mike's leg. Wagging his tiny tail, he humped and panted erotically.

Holy shit. Mike's eyes widened. Shaking his leg frantically, he danced around the room while trying to free himself from the dog's nirvanas grip. He braced against a table while kicking his leg; but Booger, enjoying the ride, hung on tight.

"Booger, that's not nice." Holding two full wine glasses, Coco trotted toward them. After hurriedly setting one of the glasses on the table, she slapped Booger on the top of his head, during which the wine in the glass splashed down Mike's white shirt.

Booger shrunk away from his leg with a yelp and scampered out of the room with his tail-tucked between his legs.

"Oh Mike, I'm sorry!"

Hoping that he wouldn't only have to imagine this butterfingered ballerina naked tonight, he took a deep breath. He truly hoped that it would be an evening of pleasure worth the abyss of calamities that seemed to suck her in.

"Quick, take that shirt off, and I'll soak it in seltzer water." She fumbled with the buttons until she opened the shirt to reveal his muscled pecks and tight abs. Her fingers fluttered over his shoulders and down his strong arms when she slipped the shirt from his torso. Blushing, she averted her gaze to the red stain on his shirt. She wet her pink, full lips and looked into his eyes. *Good God, he's setting me on fire. Can I make it through dinner?*

Smiling, she brushed a wisp of his dark hair away from his brow. "I'll be right back."

Mike watched her trot up the stairs. His thoughts strayed to Ava's cat. He hated that cat. She was an evil furry thing. He wasn't exactly in love with Coco's Cocker Spaniel. *Go figure.*

When he spied the glass on the table, he drank down the remaining wine to wet his dry mouth.

He heard her footsteps on the stairs, and she reappeared with a shirt draped over her arm. She held up the over-sized nightshirt, which she helped him slip into. Although it was large on her, it was a quite taut for him.

Stepping back to take a look, she giggled.

He looked down and groaned. The shirt was brown with pink lettering that read:

Chocolate and Men
The Richer, The Better

"Well, it's better than nothing." She felt how the shirt clung to his firm torso and outlined every detail of his pecs and abs. "Although, nothing would be fine, too." Her hands traced his shoulders, down his arms, through his fingertips, and then lightly across the crotch of his jeans. "Come sit at the table," she whispered. "Dinner's almost ready."

Mike was feeling the heat, but he managed to ask, "What are we having?"

"It's a surprise."

"I can hardly wait."

She led him into a spacious, gourmet kitchen. The stainless steel appliances gleamed in the bright lights. The white cabinetry swooped around dark, granite counters.

Mike took a seat at the table, which was dressed in white, satin linens and delicate, fine china. The light from the crystal chandelier glinted off the silverware.

Booger scooted under the table to mope.

The kitchen was most impressive, but when he sat at the table with a fresh glass of wine, it wasn't the cabinetry that he was admiring. *Christ, she looks so damned tasty in that tight little rip-it-off-me-now dress.* He took a big gulp of wine and swallowed hard while trying to keep other hard things under wraps.

Coco carefully placed several pieces of meat into a skillet. It spit and sizzled in the hot oil. She cradled her wine glass in her fingers. "Your shirt should be ready for the dryer after dinner."

"That's fine."

He felt the squeeze of the dog latching around his shin again. *Sonofabitch.* He kicked. The dog yelped. He grinned.

Coco was attracted to this handsome man sitting at her table. She was more aroused by the fact that he didn't cancel their dinner date after she had smashed his horse trailer. *He's definitely a gentleman cowboy. How sexy is that?* Her lips curled at the thought. With a sultry gleam in her sapphire eyes, she strode toward him.

More than the meat was sizzling.

Mike knew what that look meant. *Oh, yeah, no imagination needed. The ballerina is about to do her little dance.*

She leaned over him.

While she paused to take in his hazel eyes, he could feel her breath on his face.

"I wanted to cook something fancy," she whispered, "because it makes me feel fancy." Her lips crashed against his. Her tongue searched his mouth.

He ran his fingers through her hair. Cupping her face in his hands, he kissed her back with passion.

The meat crackled in the skillet.

She ran her hands over his chest and down to his hips. Her fingers found the outline of his erection pressing against his jeans. She groped at his belt.

Kissing her neck, he slipped a sleeve of the dress off and nipped at her shoulder. Tasting her skin, he made his way hungrily down her chest.

Crunch! The force of a body wrapped around his leg broke through the lust. Booger humped and pushed, which made it impossible to ignore.

Damn it. Mike's eyes popped open. He attempted to kick the dog, but he was fastened on tight and going at it strong.

Abruptly, he became aware that Booger's love connection to his leg wasn't the biggest problem at hand.

Smoke billowed from the skillet. Flames leapt from the stove. Greasy fireballs ignited dish towels. The curtains were already ablaze.

Shoving Coco onto the table, Mike sprung to his feet.

Her face lit up with intense desire. "Oh Mike, you are naughty," she gasped.

"Coco, where's your fire extinguisher?"

"You wanna be a fireman?" She was giddy.

Booger was rapt.

Mike was exasperated. "No, your fire extinguisher! Where is it?"

Flames shot across the counter top. The smoking skillet spit sparks and fire like a cannon.

He snatched the tablecloth from under Coco and ripped it off the table. China, glassware, silver crashed and broke against the wall and on the floor. He beat the flames while dragging the horny Cocker Spaniel, still humping his leg, across the room with him.

"Call the fire department."

"Wha—" Coco tried to get a grasp on the situation.

"Nine-one-one!" Mike shrieked while thrashing the flames, kicking his leg, and cursing her calamity.

ଔ ଯ ଔ ଯ

With his belt dangling from his waist, Mike sat on the steps in front of Coco's townhouse with an oxygen mask clasped to his face, which was covered in thick, black soot. With a glazed-over, disgusted expression, he watched the fire fighters roll up the hoses, and load them into their trucks.

Neighbors gathered on the sidewalks to whisper and point. Mike wondered how many times they gathered to gossip about the catastrophic Coco.

A young fire fighter approached the steps to claim a rolled-up hose next to where he was sitting. Fixated on the nightshirt clinging to Mike's every muscle, his lips moved slightly while he read the words scrolled across his chest. Looking at him like he was a circus freak, his eyebrows rose.

Mike ripped the oxygen mask from his face. "It's not my shirt."

With a shrug and a wink, the fire fighter swooped up the hose and retreated to the fire truck.

ଔ ଯ ଔ ଯ

The full moon splashed its light over the wooden rural landscape along Ridge Road. Feeling like a total idiot, not to mention gravely let down, Mike took the long way home. He smelled like smoke, he felt like shit, and he couldn't wait to take a shower. He never got to see Coco naked. *Hell, things were heading for beyond naked if dinner hadn't exploded. Yep, it's going to be a cold shower tonight.*

He steered the truck into his driveway that was fifteen hundred feet before the main stone entrance into Westwood. After rolling along the white fences under the canopy of the oak trees, it crunched to a stop in front of his bungalow. Mike saw that the barn lights were on. Then, he noticed the time: eleven o'clock.

"What now?" He shoved the truck back into gear.

CB   ͸   CB   ͸

The barn was trashed. Broken bales of hay were half-eaten and scattered over the floor. Wheelbarrows, buckets, and pitchforks were tossed in every direction. The horses whinnied from their stalls and stomped their feet. Eric gathered what hay he could salvage; while Kate, wearing her pajamas, swept the floor. She was murmuring disparaging comments about her older brother.

Leading Charlatan toward his stall, Shane wearily shuffled up the aisle when his brother slipped through the barn door.

Mike was greeted by their stiff glares. "Not again," he sighed.

Eric glowered with his infamous I'm-going-to-skin-you-with-a-dull-knife look that used to make Mike's blood curl when he was a kid. His eyes trained on the words on the nightshirt, and then to his black sooty face. "Yep, you've got a real handle on the situation, son."

Oh yeah, there's that icy tone that always backs-up the infamous look.

Eric shoved a pitchfork into Mike's hand and marched out the door.

Feeling a tap on his shoulder, Mike turned. Kate eyes burned through him when she shoved her broom at him and followed her father.

He looked around at the huge mess that the horses had provided. Coco's firehouse calamity had followed him home, and it was burning a hole in his gut. Maybe he would have seen the humor in all this, maybe he would have laughed it off, if he had gotten to see her naked.

He was lost in the mess, disgust, and less than satisfying dinner date when he noticed Shane with a cock-eyed grin on his face.

Reading the less-than-dignified message on the woman's nightshirt that Mike was wearing. Shane's gleaming eyes met his. His grin transformed into an all-out toothy smile. "Whoa, Coco's kinda kinky."

"Shut-up."

Chuckling, Shane followed his father and his sister from the barn to leave him to the task of cleaning up.

Mike began to sweep the hay along the aisle when he noticed Charlatan stretching his neck under the gate of his stall and slapping his big lips together while trying to chomp a broken bale of hay that was just out of his reach.

Mike tossed the broom aside. "You've had enough hay for one night, don't you think?"

He pushed the horse's head back and kicked the hay aside when he realized that Charlatan was not stretching for the hay. Coco had left the bag of peppermints on the bale. When the horses broke it, the bag must have fallen behind it. The sweet peppermints were scattered amongst the hay.

Mike picked up the bag.

Charlatan's ears perked. His eyes widened. Snorting at the sound of the crinkling bag, the horse stomped his feet.

Mike's right brow lifted. His eyes narrowed. Extending his palm with a peppermint, Charlatan gulped it in. He sucked in the flavor with such replete that it was almost like he was having a damned orgasm.

Amazed at the Thoroughbred's utter bliss, Mike blinked hard. He shoved a handful of peppermints into his jeans.

The soot on his face and demeaning T-shirt stretched across his pecks were forgotten. The trashed barn was the furthest thing on his mind when he darted to the tack room and flipped on the light. He yanked an exercise saddle from among the many hanging on the tree, and grabbed a bridle from the tack rack. He hurried back to Charlatan's stall.

When he stepped inside the stall, Charlatan almost knocked him down while nuzzling his pocket hard in a feverish search for another peppermint treat. Mike was quick to oblige. While Charlatan was in his nirvanas mint trance, he tossed the saddle on the horse's back and tightened the girth.

Success. No fuss, no muss, and more importantly, no flipping. *TLC. Maybe Coco was on to something, after all. Who would have guessed?*

He had to find out for sure.

He shoved the bit in Charlatan's mouth, led him from his stall, down the aisle, and out the barn door into the cloak of night.

They walked along the winding path toward the training track. Seeping through the canopy of the trees overhead, the moonlight stalked them to illuminate the wide yawn of the track at the end of the trail.

The grey gelding was a bulldozer of a horse with a wide chest, big round hips, and good stout legs. Mike was an easy six-foot-two and weighed about one-hundred-and-ninety pounds, but he felt confident that Charlatan could carry him for one moonlit test run.

He tossed Charlatan another mint, which he caught in mid-air. No one would be around to pick his sorry ass up out of the dirt if the big gelding decided to flip-over, but his gut told him that that's not how the moonlit experiment would end.

Mike leapt into the saddle, pressed his feet into the irons, and urged Charlatan onto the track. The big horse snorted and his feet danced in the sand before he galloped into the moonbeams. His neck arched. Mike kept a tight gathered hold on the reins until he pushed his arms forward and let Charlatan have his run.

Wahoo!

Part Two

Feel the Burn

~ *Six* ~

August mornings provide a lovely prelude to autumn's crisp, refreshing air in the Allegheny Mountain region.

A breeze rustled Eric's hair while he strolled through the shed rows after leaving the cafeteria with a cardboard tray filled with coffees.

Jen Fleming tiptoed from behind to playfully loop her arm through his. A slender, attractive, middle-aged woman, Jen was the racetrack nurse. She wore her brunette tresses in a short blunt cut around her face to give her a pixie-like appearance.

Having a thing for the imposing patriarch of Westwood Stables, she was optimistic that someday he would have a thing for her as well. So far, he behaved like a charming courteous gentleman toward her. That wasn't exactly what she had in mind, but it would have do for now.

"Good morning, *Mr. West*," she chirped in a sing-song voice.

Eric smiled. "Good morning, Jen, what brings you to the lowly backside?"

"I was hoping one of those coffees might be for me."

He looked down at the coffees. There were no extras, so he plucked his cup from the tray. "This one looks about right."

Grinning, she wrapped her hands around the warm Styrofoam cup that the true gentleman gave up for her. Oh yes, she was well aware of the sacrifice. "Do you have horses racing tonight?"

"Mike has a mare in the fifth race for Coco Beardmore."

"Mmmm, what's she like?"

"Interesting, in a frightening sort of way," he answered.

"So I've heard."

They shared a quiet chuckle.

"West!" Doug O'Conner's gruff voice skittered up his spine. "You're just the man I wanna talk to." He spit an icky brown line of tobacco juice at their feet.

Eric's brows furrowed. "What's the problem?"

"That oldest boy of yours, that's what. I'm gonna kick his ass!" Doug shook his fist in his face before turning to Jen. "You watch 'em, Ms. Fleming. Them Wests ain't nothing but a bunch of horny bastards."

Her eyes widened and her lips parted. She was stunned.

Placing his open palm hard against Doug's chest, Eric forced him back a step. Through a clenched jaw, he spoke, "Why don't you calm down and tell me what's eating at you?"

"Mike came to the barn last night and had a little one-on-one with my Marge."

"With *Margie?*" Jen didn't realize she had said it out loud.

He glared at her.

Swallowing hard, she back-peddled. "She's a lovely girl."

Eric's face wrinkled with doubt when he asked, "Who said so?"

"I got my sources."

That morning, Scott had informed Doug over coffee and Copenhagen about bumping into Mike while rushing, red-faced, from the barn. He also relayed his sincere concern. Margie had seemed very guarded about her meeting with Mike and he saw her adjusting her shirt while leaving the office.

That was good enough for Doug. Mike West had done the dirty deed, and it was time for him to fess-up and pay-up.

"I asked Margie, too," Doug told Eric. "She says he was just asking questions about Coo-coo Coco's horses. She's just trying to protect him from a good ass kicking. That's what I think."

"I'm sure it was more than likely the way Margie tells it," Eric said. "Mike would never take advantage of her."

Doug's face went from smack-dab injured to insulted. "What? You think your boy is too good to take Margie for a little joy ride? I'll take you on right here, West!" He hitched his pants higher on his hips and pushed his sleeves farther up his arms.

"Relax, Doug. Give me a chance to talk to Mike before we declare all-out war." Eric wasn't into street fighting.

A crowd was beginning to gather with hopes for some cheap entertainment to add to the juicy gossip they'd just been fed. That gossip would rip through the backside within mega seconds.

With his lip jutted out, Doug stood with his feet spread apart, his jaw set, and his fists poised high for a little round of fist-a-cuffs. Scowling, he contemplated Eric's request. Feeling as though he had already tasted victory, he let his hands relax and drop to his sides.

He scrubbed his whiskers with his grimy twisted fingers. "Fair enough, West. But talk to him quick, and if my Marge is knocked-up … He's a dead man!" He surveyed the crowd listening to his boisterous threats. Satisfied with his display of command, he nodded at them. Cocking his chin high, he strutted into his barn.

Bemused, Jen turned to Eric. "What was that?"

He sighed. "I'll have to find out." Taking note of the crowd still staring at them, he took her gently by the elbow and ushered her toward his stable. "Hey, how's that coffee?"

C3 80 CR 80

Margie was terrified. Stealthily, she searched the shed rows for Mike to warn him that her father was pissed-off as hell and targeted for him. She couldn't imagine why Scott would have told him such a shameful story. *Yeah, Mike came to see me. Yeah, we were in the office. No, he didn't touch me. Damn it.*

She tried to convince her hard-headed, mule-minded, father that all Mike wanted was information about Coco's grey gelding. *But no, he has it in for the West family.*

Why even when Dr. Spears came to care for a horse, Kate had to wait outside the stable. She had never done anything wrong. She was a West, and that was reason enough for Doug.

Margie couldn't think of anything the Wests may have done to her father. Same as the rest of them, Eric West was always polite. But Doug

O'Conner hated the very sight of them. Actually, he had little use for anyone at all—especially women.

Margie fingered the pair of glasses she had clipped to her shirt that she had found in an old desk drawer at home. She thought that if she could see the words in Scott's book a little better that maybe she could read them. She crept around the corner of Westwood Stables in hope that Mike might wander out. He did with Coco at his side. Margie ducked behind the stable.

They spoke for only a moment before Coco brushed her lips over his and walked away.

Damn it.

Margie felt a presence over her shoulder and turned.

Ava West was watching, too. Her eyes were piercing. Her lips were tight and thin.

"Ava, what're you doing here?" she whispered.

Her gorgeous green eyes flickered. "I could ask you the same question. Who's that woman with Michael?"

"Coco Beardmore."

"Is that—"

"Yeah, yeah, Beardmore Industries. She's pretty and rich, and I think she's seeing Mike."

Ava's lips jutted. After the confrontation between Eric and Doug that morning, the story about Mike's roll-in-the-hay with Margie was already the hot topic. She didn't believe it for a nanosecond, but she said, "I heard you were seeing Michael."

Margie snorted. "I wish."

"I bet," Ava wryly retorted. Mike was not only out of her league; but Margie wasn't even in the same galaxy. *Yeah, he wouldn't touch you with a ten-foot pole.*

The fact remained that a beautiful blonde with a boatload of coin was seeing her ex. The Wests were very well-off, and their Thoroughbred operation was more that lucrative. *Adding a million-dollar baby to the mix? That is not good.* She still commanded a little control over her ex-hubby, and had no intention of letting go.

Flinging her auburn hair over her shoulder, Ava delved into manipulation mode. *I'll have to be sly. Not a problem. Sly Bitch is my middle name.*

Once again wondering why Ava would ever let a man like Mike go, Margie watched her walk away. *She must be crazy.* That was the only conclusion she could come to.

"Hey, Margie." Dan Quaide's husky voice came out of nowhere.

She jumped and turned toward him.

The burly horse trainer looked down at her. "Whatcha doing?"

Her mouth moved, but nothing came out for a moment. "Nothing ... I wasn't doing nothing. How ya been, Dan?" *How very brainy of me to make it look like I'm just hanging out, not peering around corners, not looking for Mike West.*

"Are you looking for the Wests?"

"No, I was just hanging around, doing nothing," She kicked a stone with her foot while appearing as casual as possible.

He tossed her an odd look, and then pulled out a condition book from the pocket of his old battered jeans. "Could you look in here for me? I need to know the day they're running the three-year-old and up mares that haven't won a race in a year. I forgot my glasses at home. I can't read a damned thing without them." He handed her the book that had the lists of races for the upcoming six weeks.

Margie's eyes widened. Her face paled. "Ya know, I forgot my glasses at home, too. Damned if I can read anything without mine."

His brows furrowed. Dan pointed out, "Margie, your glasses are right there clipped to your shirt."

Her hand found its way to the glasses. Words stuck dry in her throat. She gazed at him staring at her, like she'd grown another head. "I gotta go," she finally blurted while jogging down the shed rows toward her own stable.

~ *Seven* ~

The outdoor paddock at Keystone Downs was surrounded by a white fence, which was adorned by manicured boxwood hedges. Bifocals parked at the edge of their noses, racing enthusiasts lined the paddock with race programs in hand. They glanced up from the program picks to the Thoroughbreds being led around the paddock.

Shane led a tall lanky bay mare that pranced and tossed her bowed neck for the crowd. Mike leaned against the saddling stall with his arms crossed over his chest while watching the mare's every move.

Gauging Mike's pensive expression, Punch leaned on the opposite side of the stall. He couldn't figure why Mike was so tense. This was just another race. This mare had been leaving the other horses in the dust during morning workouts. *So, what's the problem?*

After lugging her vet box across the paddock, Kate checked out the pumped-up mare that Shane was struggling to keep under control.

"Isn't that one of Malibu Barbie's horses?" She approached Mike.

"Yep," he replied.

She searched the fence line, and then the paddock area. No Coco. "Where is Goldilocks?"

"Her name is Coco. The insurance adjustor is coming this evening."

A crooked devilish smile appeared on Kate's lips. "Will she be serving him flambé?"

In no humor, Mike tossed her a dirty look. She unsuccessfully tried to smother her chuckle.

"Are you sticking around for the race?" he asked.

She checked her cell phone. "I'm supposed to go sign for my new car."

"Ah, c'mon, it's only a few more minutes. You'll look pretty in the win picture."

She shrugged. "Well, you seem quite confident. Okay, I'll stay."

Shane led the mare to the stall. After the track valet arrived with the saddle, he steadied the nervous mare while Mike tightened the girth.

Twirling their crops through their fingers, the jockeys filed from the locker room and approached their mounts. Sebastian O'Terra rode many mounts for Westwood Stables. With a wide smile, he extended his hand to Mike. His Italian accent was heavy, but his physique was light. "Are we ready to win this one?" he asked with a great air of confidence.

"Should be a cinch."

"My thought exactly," Sebastian said. "You want me to send her, right?"

"Yep, go straight for the lead."

"Riders up!" The short chubby paddock manager hollered in his gruff, all-business voice.

After Mike gave Sebastian a leg up, the horses with their riders trotted toward the tunnel that traveled under the grandstands to open up onto the racetrack at the opposite end. Sebastian bounced along in the tiny saddle with his legs dangling at the mare's sides. He was tying the reins into a knot when they disappeared into the tunnel.

ଓ ଚ ଓ ଚ

In the grandstands, Mike, Punch, Kate, and Shane found a good spot among the patrons waiting for the horses to be loaded into the starting gate. Nervously, Mike fumbled with his binoculars until he finally parked them in front of his eyes to watch the bay mare being loaded in her post position. So far, all seemed to be going well.

He couldn't bring himself to trust Coco's horses. They were always causing one debacle or another. This bay mare seemed to be more of a follower than a leader. If she ran her race the way Mike and Sebastian had planned, she should win easily ... if ...

Frowning, Shane shoved his cell phone into his hip pocket.

"What's the matter?" Mike asked.

"Tom Mason. I've been trying to get a hold of him. He isn't answering his phone."

"Maybe he's turned tail and run."

"Can't say as I blame him after ..." He decided that was a sentence better left unfinished. After the fiasco in the swimming facility, and then the fire, it was a better idea to drop it.

The track announcer interrupted their conversation. "The horses are at their posts."

Like a freaking amateur, Mike's palms were sweating.

The bell rang. The gates burst open. The horses thrust forward from their posts.

Mike searched the stampede for Coco's bay mare, Number Six.

CB EO CB EO

At the gate, Sebastian sat on his mount. He slapped the mare with his crop, but she refused to move. He whacked her again across the rump.

Frozen wide-eyed in position, she snorted.

The gate crew watched with baffled expressions while Sebastian kicked and slapped and cursed in Italian.

Finally, one impatient member of the crew stepped forward. "C'mon, O'Terra, get her going."

"I'm trying!" Sebastian bellowed.

The ten men that made up the gate crew exchanged befuddled glances. Then, they surrounded the mare.

CB EO CB EO

Mike's jaw dropped open when he spied through his binoculars Coco's mare standing in the gate with the gate crew pushing and shoving on her rump while Sebastian slapped her with his crop. Shane sucked down the last drop from his can of soda while squinting over the top in search of the Number Six horse among the field that was now maneuvering the Clubhouse turn.

"What's going on? I thought you were gonna send her." He noticed his brother's expression.

"She's still in the gate. What the hell is Sebastian doing?" Mike fretted.

CB ED CR ED

The gate crew pushed and shoved and grunted and clucked at the obstinate mare to no avail. Finally, she shifted her weight from one hoof to the other. Optimistic that she would at last step out of the gate, the gate crew stepped back.

Instead the mare flopped down on her rump in a sitting dog position. Sebastian slid down her back to the ground into the sand. *Thump.* The gate crew was aghast.

CB ED CR ED

The horses that willingly participated in the race thundered across the finish line in front of the grandstands to a cheering crowd.

Mike wasn't cheering. He was watching his horse now being pulled and tugged by the gate crew in an effort to get her into a standing position. His face was pallid. He could feel his stomach churn.

The track announcer kept the patrons informed. "Salty Silver Sally wins by five lengths. Looks like the Number Six horse is still standing, I mean, *sitting* in the starting gate."

The John Deere tractor pulled the gate forward, to reveal the seated mare chomping on her bit like a cow on a cud. Laughing and pointing, the crowd went wild. Some even took pictures with their cell phones.

Mike cupped his forehead in his hand.

Punch grabbed the binoculars from him. He'd never seen such a display of repudiation. He thought back on Coco's grey gelding flipping over in the stall while he was trying to saddle him. Shaking his head, he lowered the binoculars to his chest. "I don't believe it." He was bewildered by the sight. "We've got *flipper* and *flopper.*"

"What the hell do I do now?" Mike dug deep into his mind's eye in search of an image of Coco stark naked. *Nope, nothing.*

The answer seemed crystal clear to Kate. "Get rid of that bimbo. She's been nothing but trouble."

"She's right, Mike," Punch said.

Certain that his brother would have a smartass comment, Mike glanced at Shane, who shrugged and gulped the last of his second can of soda before tossing it in the trash bin.

"Mike West, the gate crew requests that you claim your horse from the starting gate, please," the announcer said.

CB ED CR ED

Hidden among the hundreds of cars in the dark parking lot, Margie listened to the race that she knew Mike had a horse in on the radio in her father's truck. She hoped to talk to him after the race. She didn't want him to be caught off-guard. Doug was seething mad about something that never took place between them. After what happened during the race, she thought it best to try and warn him later.

She turned the key in the ignition and the old, rickety truck rumbled to a start. She heard a soft *bing*. Looking down on the dash, she noticed the *door ajar* light glowing in the darkness. Taking a firm hold of the handle, she shouldered the door hard and jerked it all the way open.

There was a yelp, and a hard *thump*.

Perplexed by the sound, she peered out the window to find Coco in a puddle on the pavement.

Margie jumped from the truck. "Oh my God, Coco. I'm so sorry. I didn't see you there." She grabbed her by the arm and hoisted her to her feet.

Slightly dazed, Coco was soaked from her shoulder blades to her buttocks. "I was trying to make it to see the race." Trying to focus, she rubbed her head. "Did she do good?"

Margie wasn't so sure that she wanted to be the bearer of the big flop. "Well, she could've done better," she said with a wince. "Are you okay?"

Coco ran her fingers through her hair while taking in her drenched clothing. "I think so."

Margie couldn't believe how beautiful this woman looked even when sopping wet and disheveled. Even when she hadn't been knocked to the ground and wasn't sopping wet, she always look disheveled and undone.

Envy scraped down Margie's spine, burned through her gut, and into her soul. Coco had never been anything but kind to her, and she had no right to feel badly toward her. She struggled to slash through the pit of jealousy she couldn't help but fall into.

"You should get out of those wet clothes. They're pretty filthy, too," she said while watching Coco twist and turn to gauge the damage.

"I really wanted to see Mike," she moaned.

Margie thought about the stubborn mare sitting in the starting gate. She was certain that Mike had enough to deal with at the moment. "Ahhh, I dunno. He's probably gonna be pretty busy for a while. C'mon, I've got some extra clothes at the barn." With that, she took Coco by the arm and led her to the passenger side of the truck.

☙ ❧ ☙ ❧

The O'Conner stable was dark when Margie rolled the pickup to a stop in front of the barn door.

Coco was apprehensive. "I don't think your father's going to be happy to see me, Margie." She eyed-up the stable while searching the shadows for any sign of the nasty man.

"I don't think he would be either." Margie shoved the truck in PARK. "Good thing he went home about an hour ago," she added with a wink.

Coco slid from the truck to follow Margie into the dark, shabby stable. The horses nickered quietly to Margie when she flicked on the lights. Gently, she stroked each horse's muzzle when she passed their stall while approaching the barn office. She hadn't lived a charmed life in a big house with closets full of designer clothes, social mixers, or traveling to Europe on a whimsy vacation. No, Margie's life was hard, full of work, toil, and then more work. With all that in mind, Coco found herself admiring the woman. *She's unassuming. She knows who she is. Although she has so little, she loves what she has. And those are qualities well-worth possessing. Qualities that have escaped so many people, including me.*

Margie opened a large storage bin in the corner of the office and pulled out a pair of clean Lee jeans; and an aged, but clean, T-shirt. Looking at Coco's jeans and her soiled silk blouse, she was embarrassed by the offering. "They're not fancy, but they'll get you home."

Coco smiled. "They'll do just fine. Thank you so much for your kindness. You have the most beautiful eyes. You really do, Margie."

Margie was unsure if the gorgeous goddess was offering a pity compliment or if she was sincere. It didn't matter. Her generous words filled her with a moment of rare replete.

☙ ❧ ☙ ❧

What a lousy night. Mike drug his weary body from his pickup and shuffled across the stone patio to the kitchen door. He was feeling used, abused, and well spent. The image of Coco's mare sitting in the starting gate went round and round in his mind. The image of Coco naked in his bed? Not happening. He was absolutely sure that there would be a forgive and forget scenario involved somewhere in this disaster.

"Hi, Mike. How did it go tonight?" Coco's tender voice jolted him to attention. There she was in that little, black have-hot-sex-with-me-now dress. She was thankful that she had caught him. After her debacle in the parking lot, Coco had rushed home to change into something more … alluring than Margie's barn clothes.

Feeling a bit flushed and noticing Mike's apprehension, she decided he might need a little encouragment after their last dinner date. "I won't go near your stove and you can pour." Smiling, she held up a bottle of wine. She lowered her voice to an inviting, sultry murmur. "I want to make-up for the other night."

She tenderly raked her fingers through his hair, down his neck, and across his square jaw. She pressed her mouth against his and let her tongue caress his lips before she pulled away.

After all the calamities, he wanted to tell her he was too tired, that he was a coward and wary to even go inside the house with her; but before he could muster the words, she took him by the hand and guided him through the door. She had a "do things to me" look in her eyes. He was rendered helpless.

She led him through his small kitchen with oak cabinetry, a bistro-style table and chairs beneath an arched window that looked out over the white barns with blue tin roofs and white fences. "Cute kitchen, it makes me want to bake cookies." When he pitched a warning look, she giggled. "Teasing—I'm teasing."

She found his living room with the stone fireplace. A *simple décor for the gorgeous, gentlemanly cowboy.* She pulled him down onto the sofa.

Mike was beyond helping himself. The way she tugged at his shirt with the look in those blue eyes, and the passion in her kisses on his mouth and neck while she unzipped his Levis had him forgetting how tired he was, his trashed trailer, the burnt kitchen, and her flipping/flopping horses. It was time to sit-back, relax, and let the "trainer with benefits" package finally kick-in. *It's about damned time.*

His strong hands gently smoothed down her neck, and over her shoulders and luscious firm breasts. He looked into her enticing eyes while he slipped the dress from her shoulders to expose the sexy black satin and lace bra. Her hand slipped inside his jeans to stroke the hard length of him.

Bang!

Bang!

Bang!

Their heads jerked toward the kitchen. Someone was knocking on the screen door.

Seriously?

"Michael, are you in there? Hello ..." Ava's voice carried through the house.

Mike's head dropped to his chest. *What the hell is she doing here?* boomed through his brain.

Hastily, Coco pulled her dress back into position. "Who is that?"

It didn't matter. Ava stepped through the threshold of the kitchen, and was now standing in the living room.

Pulling his jeans together, he could see in Coco's eyes that something was amiss. He was afraid to look, but he had to. Slowly, he turned toward Ava.

"Oh, I'm sorry, Michael. I didn't know you had company." Looking like red-hot desire, Ava was dressed in the exact same little, black have-your-way-with-me-now dress that Coco was wearing. There she stood with her auburn hair draped over her shoulders. He felt like he was about to star in a very bad porn flick.

That wasn't happening—not in this life anyway. He knew Ava.

"What's going on, Ava?" Suspicion filled his tone and his narrowed eyes.

Coco whispered in his ear, "Should I go?"

"No," he replied embarrassingly fast. He wasn't letting his "trainer with benefits" get lost in the shuffle—not this time. He jumped up and, as gently as an aroused man can, he took Ava by the arm.

"Coco," he called over his shoulder, "Make yourself comfortable. I'll be right back."

CB &O CR &O

He ushered Ava through the kitchen directly to the patio behind the house. Once he felt they were safely out of ear-shot, he whipped the stunning red-head around to face him.

She was wearing her sultry green bedroom eyes—the one's he could never resist—the one's she used to get exactly what she wanted from him. He felt himself waning. He wanted to pull her close and press his lips over hers. Shit, he wanted to put his lips everywhere. She still owned a corner of his soul. He was feeling pissed at himself for it. *Not today. I've forgiven and forgotten. Forgave my stupidity. Forgot her existence. Remember?* Still, there she was looking hot in that little take-me-now-I'm-yours dress. *Damn to hell.*

"What are you doing here, Ava?" he demanded in a low and deliberate tone.

Her eyes and her voice were filled with the sweet innocence of a kitten. "I heard you had a bad day. I came to cheer you up." She purred while feathering her fingers through his open shirt and across his chest. "I didn't realize you had company. Someone new?" Using her master manipulation skills, her index finger traced the buttons on his shirt down to his jeans while poking it through a button hole to circle his navel. It was gentle, sensual, and driving.

The muscles in his abs contracted and his spine tensed at the caressing tease of her fingernail.

Ava knew she would get this kind of a response. Her touch always made him liquefy. She could see the melt-down well underway. *Game over. I own him. I can have him here and now on the patio while Miss Rich Blonde Bombshell's waiting for him in the living room.* Not that that was necessarily a bad thing. Sex with Michael was great. It was the one thing about their marriage she relished, maybe even missed. *When this man takes his clothes off he's a study in hot-damn-amazing. When things get hot, he's as hot as they get—blazing.* But she had to keep it at a distance, or the control she wielded could possibly wilt.

Mike was waning, damn it, the way he always did when she touched him that way. *Pull it together. Today? Ava came to cheer me up today?* "What about your boyfriend? Lugowski?" he asked while trying to reconcile with his senses.

She took in a long, deep breath, and then released it with a long, sultry sigh. She swept a stray auburn strand from her cheek. Her emerald gaze dragged to meet his. Shrugging her tasty little shoulder, she licked her lips.

Ahhh, that's what I thought. He smelled a covert operation in the worst sort of way—Ava's way. Not today. He was completely reconciled with his forgive-forget strategy.

Without further ado, he grabbed her hand before it went any further; before it went any further south; before he let her do what she was so good at doing—getting her way with him. His voice was hoarse and quiet and edging on remorse, but his eyes held steadfast on hers.

"You better be on your way, Ava. Thanks for dropping by."

03 80 03 80

Coco had no clue who the pretty redhead was, but it didn't go unnoticed that her abrupt appearance rattled Mike. He assured her it wasn't a problem. She had her doubts. Sighing, she busied herself with a look around the sparsely decorated room. The spiral stairs that led to an open loft summoned her interest. She slowly climbed the charming twirly stairs. When she reached the loft, she peered over the railing to the openness of the living room below. Splashed with dark hues of orange, black, and a subtle stroke of azure; two long Indian throw-rugs filled the loft's oak floor.

Nice touch, cowboy.

She wandered into the first door on the left. The room smelled of a man's musky outdoorsman cologne. The walls were painted with a soft gray. Her attention was drawn to the king-size bed that had a fluffy gray comforter with a dark charcoal stripe spread over it. Large charcoal Euro pillows with the dark black swirls were tossed near the headboard. The picture that hung over the bed drew her near. It was an impressively framed and matted photograph of the great Secretariat crossing the finish line at the 1973 Kentucky Derby. It was signed by Big Red's jockey, Ron Turcotte.

Jackpot! This is the cowboy's bedroom.

She made her way to a dresser near the window. There was a bottle of Old Spice, a penknife, and several racing programs piled off to one side. She was now certain that this room was Mike's. With that, her lips curled.

She tossed several pillows to the floor and pulled the comforter down. *The sexy redhead will be out of luck. Too bad.*

She slipped the little black dress from her shoulders and let it flutter from her body to the floor. The black satin bra and lacey black g-string soon landed on top of the dress. She was looking forward to running her fingers over his firm chest. She tried to imagine how the cowboy, engorged, would look standing naked before her with a "come on" look in his eyes. *Oh yes, the cowboy scenario is working just fine.* She searched the room in hopes of finding a cowboy hat. A Stetson would be the icing on her carnal cowboy cake.

CB   ED   CR   ED

The front door opened. Shane poked his head inside the cottage. "Mike, yo, Mike. You in here?"

The lights were on, so he crossed the living room to check the kitchen. *Not there.* He went back through the living room. He heard a rustling in the bedroom upstairs. Shane trotted up the stairs and opened Mike's bedroom door.

He took in a breath and was unable to release it. Filled with a wondrous sight, his eyes widened.

There she was, Coco ... completely, incredibly, naked.

She was extraordinary. Her full firm breasts hung high. Her nipples were a dusty rose, and her long blonde locks swept across her beautiful defined shoulders. Her tiny rib cage gently eased down to her shapely hips. She was slickly waxed, Brazilian, and she had a tiny tattoo next to her ...

Lord have mercy.

Grabbing the comforter to strap it around her nakedness, Coco screamed.

Shane jumped back. "I'm sorry! I'm so sorry!" His voice was high-pitched while he backed out of the room with his right arm extended out in case she would decide to hurl the lamp. "I ... I was looking for Mike ..."

The door slammed in his face.

He gulped in a breath while savoring the incredible image. Then he turned to bump face-to-face with big brother.

"What the hell is going on?"

"I was looking for you. I thought you were in her, I mean there. She was freaking naked."

Mike's eyes were like lasers burning through Shane's face, *"Naked?"* he spluttered.

"Oh, yeah," Shane breathed. *"Naked."*

The bedroom door whipped open with a gust causing them to flinch.

Coco's dress was askew. Hopping on one foot while fumbling into her heels, she glared into Shane's eyes. "I'm not into weird stuff," she announced. "I'm going home, Mike. Maybe that redhead is a little more adventurous."

"There was a redhead too?" Shane was most impressed with his brother's evening.

"*Ava* ..." Mike growled.

"Ouch." Shane cringed.

"Coco wait—" Mike said.

"No, Mike, it just doesn't feel right ... good night."

Coco grasped the railing and paddled down the stairs. After stumbling, she managed to regain her balance and finally reached the bottom. While tugging at her dress, she made haste for the door and slammed it behind her.

From over the railing up in the loft, the West brothers watched her harried retreat.

After the reverberation from the slam of the door quieted, Shane turned to his older brother. The memory of her was fresh in his mind. "She was *totally* unbelievable, dude." He was still in awe of her sumptuous body.

"Shut up."

~ *Eight* ~

They weren't totally convinced. Eric and Punch stood with their arms crossed over their chests while listening to Mike make his case.

He patted Charlatan, also known as "Flipper", while he explained, "I've discovered what makes this guy tick." When Mike tugged open a package of peppermints, Charlatan's eyes grew big, his nostrils flared, and he snorted impatiently. "Peppermints."

Eric and Punch exchanged befuddled glances.

The left side of Eric's lip tucked. His brow raised. "Did you take him to the track?"

"That's today's chore. He stands perfectly to be saddled. No more flipping thanks to these peppermints." He held up the bag: Exhibit A.

Charlatan stomped his feet with irritation. Mike flipped him a mint. The gelding caught it in mid-air and retreated back into his stall while sucking on it like a spoiled child with a lollipop.

Eric's mouth opened slightly at the sight of the contented gelding.

"So all we have to do is feed him the peppermints while he's being saddled, and he won't flip?" Punch wanted to make sure he was seeing what he thought he was seeing.

"That's how it looks to me," Mike said.

"What about the other one?" Eric asked with a stiff tone. Exhibit B.

"Do you mean Flopper?" The confidence in his voice disappeared.

What does one do with a horse that sits down, and just plain refuses to race? Mike was totally perplexed by the predicament His father's staunch stare felt heavy. "I'm still working on that one. Look, I'll take Charlatan to the track for a test drive, and then I'm gonna enter him this weekend."

"Speaking of the track," Eric said, "I need to talk to you about Mar–"

"Dad, have you heard from Tom Mason lately?" Shane interrupted them. "I can't raise him on his cell."

"No, keep trying. We want to get that horse of his on a program ASAP," he said before turning back to Mike. "I had an interesting conversation with Doug—"

"Oh, by the way, Coco's here. She's outside looking at Kate's new car," Shane said.

Mike wilted against the wall. "I really don't have time for her this morning—not if I want to get this gelding to the track."

"I'll talk to her," Eric said.

"Thanks, Dad. I'm going out the back." He whipped Charlatan from the stall and started toward the door at the far side of the barn. He hesitated. "Did you want to talk to me about something?" he called back to his father.

"See me as soon as you get back."

Cʒ ʂ Cʁ ʂ

Coco circled the radiant red convertible Mustang. She ran her fingers over the shining chrome and peered in at the black leather seats. "Oh, it's beautiful, Kate."

"Thanks. It was worth all the extra hours I've been putting in at the track."

Coco was baffled. "Your father didn't buy this?"

"I'm a big girl. I can buy my own car, thank you."

"Mmmm." She noticed the classic silver galloping Mustang hood ornament. "I didn't know they had these anymore."

"They don't," Kate said. "It was a special purchase from a classic car dealer. I had it mounted. Cost me a small fortune, but it was so worth it."

Kate glanced at the silver Lexus SUV parked near the barn door. "Where'd you get the Lexus?" She hitched her chin toward the luxury vehicle.

"Oh, that's Daddy's. Mine's in the shop," she giggled nervously. "I'm sure you know why."

Unamused, Kate smirked.

"Sharp car, isn't it?" Eric's voice made the girls turn.

"Beautiful," Coco said.

"Mike had to go to the track with your horse this morning," he began the smooth lie. "So I'm afraid he's not here."

Quite impressed with her father's fib, Kate bit her lip.

"Oh, I wanted to talk to him about last night. I'll see him later, I'm sure." She smiled. "Love the car, Kate. Not a scratch on her."

Coco climbed into the Lexus, started the engine, pushed the gear shift into DRIVE, and depressed the gas at the same time her phone announced the arrival of a text message.

"Oh, good." Hoping the call was from Mike, she reached into her Gucci bag for the cell, but it slipped through her fingers and onto the floor. She kept her left hand on the steering wheel while she stretched, and stretched while wiggling her fingers to retrieve it.

Out of the blue, she heard Eric's panicked voice. "Watch out!"

She snatched the cell from the floor and sat up in time to see him shove Kate out of the path of the Lexus when it slammed into the side of the brand-new, hard-earned Mustang.

Watching in horror, Eric and Kate lay on the ground while the Lexus pushed the Mustang a solid seven feet—squealing, tearing metal, and twisting the whole way.

ᘓ ᘔ ᘒ ᘕ

Shane rushed into the barn office to snatch up the ringing phone on the desk. "Hello? Hey, Mr. Mason, I'm so glad you called—" He barely got the words out of his mouth when he heard a terrible commotion outside. Narrowing his eyes, he raised his chin to peer out the window across the room. That's when the barn wall came crashing in.

Coco had shoved the Lexus into reverse to escape the Mustang but had pressed down too hard on the accelerator. The back-end of the SUV burst through the solid oak planking. The win pictures that once hung in tidy rows of victory were launched to scatter through the air.

Shane vaulted over the desk to take cover from the projectiles flying over his head to hit the wall behind him and collapse a metal shelving unit on top of him.

Silence followed. Smoke billowed from the vehicle that was now the centerpiece of the office.

Sliding to a stop in the doorway, Punch peered in with round, wide eyes. "Shane, where are you?" Coughing, he waded through the debris, while batting at the ashen smoke.

Waving his hand in front of his face, Shane coughed while climbing out from under the shelves.

Punch pitched rubble aside before grabbing him by the arm. "You okay?"

"Yeah, yeah, I'm okay." Then he saw it. "Coco?"

The door of the Lexus slowly opened with a squeal. Timidly, Coco emerged.

"Oh, yeah, Coco," Punch said.

CB &O CR &O

The thick ashen smoke filled the hole where the lame vehicle was jammed.

Eric pulled Kate from the ground "Good God, Coco." He dashed toward the SUV and skidded to a stop when Punch delivered her from the wreckage. Covered in ashy dust, Shane was close behind.

"Are you all right?" Eric was relieved to see everyone in one piece.

"Oh, Mr. West, I am so very, very sorry." Weeping openly, she cupped her hand over her mouth.

Shell-shocked, Kate stared at her mangled Mustang. Her lips moved, but she was unable to forms words. Her cheeks burned red and her eyes filled with fire. "Shit! Shit! Shit!" She scrambled toward the mutilated car. Her mouth dangled open and nostrils flared until her temper reached crescendo. "What the hell is the matter with you?" she wailed.

Coco couldn't answer. Visions of Mike's trashed trailer, and the scorched kitchen slammed through her head.

What is wrong with me? Am I a walking disaster area? Good God, I'm a bona-fide klutz.

Never once did Mike call her names or demand sexual compensation for the torture she realized she had wielded upon him. He was a gentleman. A genuine gentlemanly cowboy.

Rare.

She was joggled back into the moment when an object whizzed past her head.

Shane and Punch ducked. Kate had chucked the classic hood ornament from the Mustang. It smashed through the windshield of the Lexus. The security system screamed.

Clutched by alarm, Coco looked up. Poor Kate was beyond soothing. She marched around her maimed car while barking disparaging words at Coco's intelligence.

Punch tenderly touched Coco's arm.

Turning to the huge compassionate black man, she shivered.

"I think you should go home," he suggested.

Her face was wet with tears. When she looked into his face, she saw that Punch felt sorry for her, but there was something else there. Behind the empathy, she also saw the word "klutz".

Oh yes, he has the same look in his eyes that Mike had the night the kitchen caught on fire; and that Henry had in his eyes the day I smashed his brand new Bentley Mulsanne into his vintage Ashton Martin. It screams, "Bumbling klutz!" She hated that look, and she needed to find a way to eradicate it forever, and soon.

She wiped the tears from her cheeks. "Is Daddy's Lexus drivable?" she mumbled through quivering lips.

Punch glanced over his shoulder at the new embellishment wedged in the barn wall. *No way. How is she going to break the news to Daddy? Then again, I imagine Daddy is already accustomed to Coco's catastrophes.*

"I'll drive you," he told her.

☙ ❧ ☙ ❧

Mike led "Flipper", Charlatan, back into Westwood stables at Keystone Downs. Sebastian O'Terra had taken the gelding for a gallop with great success. While Sebastian fed him peppermints, he had been an angel while being saddled, and he turned in a time that was most impressive, indeed. Charlatan trotted into the stall after Mike slapped him on the rump. He let out a sigh of relief. *A simple remedy for a huge problem. Perfect.*

A nanosecond later, *BAP!* His jaw slammed sideways and his head lobbed against the stall door. Almost to his knees, he grabbed the wall to steady himself.

"I've been waiting for you, boy," a familiar gruff voice rang out beyond the white stars that were dancing in front of his eyes.

Mike shook his head. The stars cleared in time for him to duck when Doug swung a pitchfork in his immediate direction. The pitchfork bounced off the wall above his head. Doug heaved it over his shoulder to prep for another blow.

Wide eyed and snorting, the horses jumped to the back of their stalls.

Crouching low, Mike managed to maneuver around the man swinging the fork back and forth madly over his head. "What the hell's the matter with you, O'Conner?" He backed down the aisle while dodging the prongs of the pitchfork that was jabbing and stabbing toward his chest.

"You ain't getting away with what you done to my Marge! You took that sweet woman's virginity, and now I'm gonna take it outta your hide!" Doug bellowed like an old hillbilly at a shotgun affair. He swung the fork.

Mike ducked again, but his mind was racing. "I don't know what you're talking about. I never touched Margie."

"You damned Wests, you're not only womanizing pigs, you're cowards!" Filled with malevolent rage, he wrapped his arthritic fingers around the handle so tightly that his crooked knuckles looked as though they would rip through the weathered and cracked skin.

Mike grabbed for the pitchfork. Doug whipped it down to smack his hand and wound up for another bout of blows. Ducking and dodging, Mike sucked back. He was running out of real estate, and soon Doug would have him backed against the wall—literally.

"I don't know what the hell you're talking about. Now put down that damned fork!"

"I'll put the fork down when you've paid for what you took!"

"I didn't take anything!"

Doug wasn't interested in reason. Mike really didn't want to tackle the old guy, and he didn't want a broken hip added to his mounting laundry list of "forgive and forget" situations. But the wall was closing in, and so was that damned pitchfork. Tackling Doug was rapidly becoming the viable option.

"You violated my Marge!"

Hokay, enough is enough. Need to lay my cards on the table, and spell it out in a way that the old crotchety coot will understand. Doug swung the fork again, but this time Mike was ready, he grabbed the pitchfork from the old man's hand and snapped it over his knee. The crack of the handle breaking in two, and the frustration on Mike's face made Doug cower.

Out of sheer agitation, Mike pointed the broken jagged handle at him. "Listen up, Doug. I wouldn't touch Margie with a freaking ten foot pole!"

"Dad!" Margie dashed in from the end of the barn.

Tears filling her eyes and streaming down her cheeks, she stared at Mike. The image of her perfect Mike West shattered and fell into mangled fragments of her heart around the pedestal from which he had tumbled.

Her voice quivered with hurt. "Mike didn't do anything wrong. He never touched me." She glared through her tears into his eyes. "He would never get close enough to touch the likes of me. Now, you've gotta get it outta your head."

Doug's wicked daggers had been exchanged with fear. "C'mon, Dad." Margie tugged her father down the aisle to drag him out the door.

Biting down on his lip, Mike took in a deep, ashamed breath.

ଓ ଉ ଓ ଉ

Punch threw the huge, bay gelding, Disturbia, an armful of hay and watched the well muscled horse dig in. He patted him on the neck before he meandered up the aisle to turn off the lights for the night. The barn was dark. Martina McBride's voice filtered through the radio to fill the dimness. A low glow from the office sifted down the aisle. Surprised that he wasn't the only one left, he checked it out.

He found Mike leaning a hip against the desk while staring at the boarded-up wall and the huge pile of debris swept in the middle of the floor.

What a mess.

Relaxing against the door jamb, Punch folded his massive arms over his chest. "Eh, Eric was talking about putting a bigger window in anyway."

Mike pitched a broken mug into the pile. "She's a real live train wreck, isn't she?"

"Yep."

"Kate isn't speaking to me. Dad thinks I'm an irresponsible jerk, and Shane ... well, he's just Shane."

"Don't forget O'Conner. He thinks you're a pervert." Punch urged a crooked smile out of him.

"A *womanizing* pervert."

"So, what're you gonna do?"

Mike felt a snarl of regret churning in his gut. He hated himself for scaring poor Doug half-to-death. Add to that, blurting out such a grisly insult and seeing the result of his damning words in Margie's dark teary eyes. He didn't know she was there. That was no excuse. *Yep, this is turning into a huge forgive and forget state of affairs: Ava, Coco, and now Margie.*

He'd hit the trifecta.

Sliding onto the desk, he took a deep confident breath and looked Punch square in the eye. "I'm gonna race Charlatan tomorrow night. Then, I'm gonna tell Miss Beardmore to get out of Dodge."

~ *Nine* ~

Coco sat at her vanity filled with angst. The palms of her hands were sweating.

Booger's ears perked. In need of her attention, he let out a frustrated grouse. When he saw it was of no use, the dejected Spaniel flopped to the floor to pout.

Indecision rolled through her. *How can I do this to my gentlemanly cowboy? How can I not show up for Charlatan's race?* She feared that her horse would flip when Mike tried to saddle him, and then her cowboy would wield that look at her again: the klutzy-Coco look. She couldn't bear it anymore. She couldn't stand those looks anymore.

The gelding had flipped over several times when Doug attempted to saddle him, but she had surmised that the horse was threatened by the crotchety trainer's nasty demeanor. *Who could blame him?* Then, when Charlatan flipped for Mike and Punch, it shook her confidence in that conclusion.

The purple whisper of twilight seeped through her bedroom curtains. She dropped her elbows onto the vanity and put her face into her hands.

Perhaps I should stop Charlatan from racing all together. Maybe I should call the racing office and tell them that I've fired Mike as my trainer, and he isn't to enter the paddock with Charlatan.

Expelling a sigh, she realized that that would only result in a different look from the cowboy: frustration, anger, and possibly even hate. She couldn't bear to see that in his eyes.

Mike had a plan, and she hoped it would work.

Glancing down at Booger, she gently stroked his head.

Taking in a deep breath, she decided to call Mike after the race. It was a cowardly decision at best, but it was the only one she could muster.

$\infty \quad \infty \quad \infty \quad \infty$

Charlatan never looked so magnificent. Mike had instructed the groom to brush him to a laser sheen, and braid his mane.

Wide-eyed and ready to rumble, the gelding burst into the paddock at the end of Shane's lead.

Striking his usual pose, Mike leaned against the saddling stall with his arms folded over his chest while watching the gelding, the patrons eyeing him up, and the other Thoroughbreds high-stepping around the paddock.

His plan was to feed Charlatan peppermints while he was being saddled to keep him from rearing up and flipping over. He reached back to his hip pocket to make sure the bag of peppermints was still there. *Check.*

"Hey, West!" Doug's voice ripped up his spine like a chainsaw. "What's it gonna be tonight? Flip or flop?" The cantankerous old trainer shouted at him while passing Mike's stall. He expelled an obnoxious laugh followed by a croaky nicotine cough.

What an asshole.

Looking like an old, well-used, rag doll, Margie walked by carrying the bridle for the horse her father was running in the same race.

"Margie," Mike called to her.

She seriously considered ignoring him; but, to her aversion, she couldn't. *Damn it.* He was Mike West, un-ignorable, hot-as-hell, and sexier than any sin that she'd love to commit. Hating herself for feeling that way, she wished so damned bad that she could be resolute and stroll past with her nose in air and not regard him in any way. *Well, so much for that plan.*

"Good luck, Mike," she politely said while avoiding eye contact.

"Thanks, Margie. I need it."

"Oh, I dunno, Sebastian told me that he thinks he can win with that grey." She continued on.

Mike gently touched her arm. Her breath caught. *Dear God, how I wish I wasn't wearing a long sleeved shirt, so I could feel the warmth of his hand directly on my skin.*

"I'm sorry for what I said, Margie. I didn't mean it."

She gazed into those wonderful, mysterious, hazel eyes that always made her heart thump and the butterflies in her stomach whip into action. *I'm not going to let you get away with it—not this time.*

"Yeah, you did," she said. "Folks always say what they mean when they're pushed."

He was taken aback. It was true, and she knew it.

Tending her father's demands and his racehorses, Margie had lived her entire thirty-three years on the backside of Keystone Downs. She wasn't well traveled, well read, or even well spoken; but she knew the truth when she heard it, and she damned well knew a lie when she heard one, too.

Mike really was sorry. He regretted the words the minute they had come out of his mouth. Or was it that he regretted them when he realized Margie had heard them? *How many times had I said that I wouldn't touch Margie O'Conner with a ten-foot pole—and meant it.*

Suddenly, he felt a playful swat on his shoulder. "Eh, forget it," she said, "I forgive you."

"Margie, where's that damned bridle?" Doug bellowed across the paddock.

Smiling at him, she turned and did what she did best—obey her father's commands. She trotted toward him with the freshly-cleaned bridle extended out in front of her.

Forgive and forget? Just like that? It's that simple for this simple woman. Not so with the other, beautiful, complicated women in my life. Maybe that's the crux of my problem.

"Hey, Mike, we saddling this bad boy or what?" Shane called out.

Jolted back into the moment at hand, Mike turned.

Tapping his foot, the tiny saddle slung over his arm; the valet had an impatient expression on his face.

Mike grabbed the bag of peppermints from his pocket and tossed them to Shane.

"Keep him happy," he instructed.

Shane fed him a peppermint. The valet tossed the saddle onto Charlatan's back and Mike tightened the girth. The gelding savored the mint and looked for more, which Shane gladly delivered.

Twirling his crop through his fingers, Sebastian arrived at the stall. "What's the game plan?" he asked with a confident grin.

"Send him," Mike said.

"That's what I was hoping you'd say."

"Riders up!" The paddock manager's voice sliced through the sound of horses fussing, the patrons along the fence deliberating, and the murmur of last minute instructions from trainers to jockeys.

Mike gave Sebastian a leg up. Shane threw his brother a bracing glance when the gelding tossed his head.

"I've got him." Mike took the lead and guided Charlatan into the parade of Thoroughbreds that were trotting toward the tunnel. Humming a tune, Sebastian bounced along in the saddle while tying the reins in a knot. Trusting, his legs dangled casually at the gelding's sides when they drew closer to the long, dimly lit, dank tunnel.

The echo of hooves clambering on the pavement, and the Spanish chatter bouncing off the walls brought Charlatan's ears straight-up. His eyes were like pure white saucers. His nostrils flared, he snorted into Mike's ear so hard that his hair blew in the horse's hot breath.

Stroking the gelding's neck, Mike tugged at the lead while whispering, "Easy boy, take it easy, whoa now." He reached into his pocket for the peppermints—only to realize that he had given them to Shane.

Charlatan whinnied, stomped his feet, and tossed his head.

Mike's eyes trained on the opening of the tunnel. It seemed like it was five miles away. Bracing for trouble, he glanced over his shoulder and past several horses. Doug and Margie were walking alongside their sorrel gelding. Entering the tunnel, Shane tossed a peppermint into his mouth while talking with another trainer. *Shit, he's too far away to call to.*

Charlatan's eyes were now bulging with anxiety. Whinnying and snorting, he popped his front feet off the ground.

Sebastian snapped to attention. "What's up with him?"

Too late.

Rearing up, Charlatan danced backward on his hind legs. Grabbing a frock of mane, Sebastian managed to stay on for the first round.

"Jump!" Mike yelled when the gelding came down.

Charlatan pushed back up and flipped over backward. Sebastian vaulted from the saddle, smashed against the wall, and fell to the floor where he lay motionless.

Panic erupted throughout the tunnel. Whirling, horses dropped their riders to the ground. Grappling at the leads, the horse handlers tried to keep control. A huge bay gelding yanked back to break loose from his handler. Knocking people to the ground, he ran free through the confusion.

Shane tried to push his way past the panicked handlers, trainers, and horses to get to Mike, but the gap closed tight and shoved him back.

More violently hysterical, Charlatan scrambled to his feet and reared to punch out at Mike, who clung to the lead until it snapped. Mike tumbled backward to the ground. Fright filled and out of control, the gelding ran madly toward the end of the tunnel.

Margie plastered herself against the wall and slid past the confusion until she reached Mike, who was scrambling to his feet.

The world was whipping around him in a blur of horses, people, and ricocheting hysteria off the curved, tunnel walls. His fists were clenched at his sides, and his face was flushed with agitation.

Margie's tender hand squeezed his shoulder. He turned to find himself face-to-face with that unattractive gaunt face with the oversized nose. Her dark almond-shaped eyes, filled with empathy, caught his attention. She was ready to lend him a hand in a turbulent situation. Her calm voice was soothing. "You're too riled up to deal with Charlatan. Stay with Sebastian, I'll get the horse." Dodging hysterical horses and frantic people, she darted through the tunnel.

Gulping for air while reaching for someone's hand—anyone's hand, Sebastian regained consciousness.

Mike clasped it tightly. "Bad?"

Sebastian grunted. He held his torso with one hand while the other lay limp beside him. "Stuff's broken, don't know what for sure."

"Stay still. The medics are coming."

At least, Mike hoped so. Most of the horses were now being cleared from the tunnel, but Charlatan was running around the racetrack. He could hear the fans clapping and laughing. They were unaware of the dire situation in the tunnel below them.

~ *Ten* ~

Once again Mike found himself driving the long way home while contemplating life's twists and turns—and the occasional flip-over.

Someone once told him that if you wanted to hear God laugh—tell Him your plans. It seemed like God was having one hell of a long belly roller ever since he bumped into Coco Beardmore that morning at Keystone Downs and claimed her horses from Doug O'Conner.

Maybe God created her as an experiment to see how much of a sense of humor men can pull out of their asses when faced with a gorgeous goddess plagued with disaster. I can picture Him up in Heaven, smacking His knee while hooting and shaking His head.

Funny, very funny.

Glancing down at his cell phone resting on the seat, he could see there were several messages from Coco in his voice mail. An aching knot of tension formed between his eyes. *Forgive and forget: Forgive myself for letting this go too far, and forget ... who the hell am I kidding? How can I forgive myself for letting this bombshell version of Calamity Jane blur my decisions? How can I forget that Sebastian is in a hospital bed with possibly months of physical therapy ahead?*

Mike had graduated to the superfecta.

The sun was cresting the hills behind his family's home when he drove through the stone entrance of Westwood. The heavy dew glittered where it bled from the massive oaks that cradled the house. Mike rolled the pickup to stop, dragged his fingers through his dark hair and laced them together on top of his head. He closed his eyes and listened to the morning DJ on the radio tell a really bad joke.

☙ ❧ ☙ ❧

The morning light gleamed through the dining room window. Sipping his coffee, Eric wondered if Mike was home from the hospital and how Sebastian was.

It's a risk every time a jockey swings a leg over a horse. Anything can happen between the paddock and the finish line. That it happened under Westwood's watch bothered the shit out of him.

Kate carried a plate of pancakes from the kitchen and placed it in the middle of the table. They heard the kitchen door slam. Looking like he'd been dragged by a truck, Mike strolled into the dining room. She poured him a cup of coffee, which he took from her with a thin smile.

"How's Sebastian?" Eric shot him a look over his coffee cup.

While he was a grown man of thirty-three, Mike recognized the reprimand in his father's stare. He took a quick sip of the hot coffee and sighed. "Broken collar bone, three ribs, and a wrenched knee." He sank into a chair. "I can't believe how stupid I was."

The guilt that blonde wielded on her older brother cut like a knife. Kate became painfully aware that he was looking for something in Coco stripped from him by the red-headed whore he had married. Her heart ached for him. "You weren't stupid, Mike. You did everything you could to cure that horse."

"Obviously, I failed."

"Where was Betty Boobs last night?" Kate asked.

"No show."

Eric set his cup on the table, and broached the subject that he'd been dreading, "Mike, don't tell me you have feelings for her. Do you?"

"Yeah, like a bee sting on my ass." He sat back hard against the chair. "No, I think I was infatuated with—"

"Her boobs?" Shane snorted from the doorway.

Mike shrugged and cocked his head.

Kate rolled her eyes. "Nice. It's always a good idea to take on clients based on their cup size."

"Seemed like a good idea to me," Shane said with a smile. "By the way, Tom Mason called this morning. Seems he's been in Punta Cana visiting a friend."

"Hmmm, I feel another set of nuptials coming on," Eric said.

"Maybe. Anyway, he wants to come see the horse swim this morning."

Eric pitched an uncompromising gaze at Mike. "It's time to send Miss Beardmore packing. Do it before Tom gets here. We don't need anymore mishaps."

"Seriously, it would be nice to send Mr. Mason home with his vehicle in one piece," Kate said.

"Don't worry," Mike assured them. "She's as good as gone."

CB ED CR ED

Sunshine glinted off the water through the arched windows that lined the perimeter of the equine swimming area. The pump hummed, and the water lapped against the sides of the pool like a gentle lullaby.

Tom Mason took his sunglasses from his tanned face and placed them on his head while being careful not to mess his smooth, slicked-back, dark hair. He squinted to allow his dark brown eyes to acclimate to the inside.

"Eric ... Eric ... is anyone here?" He made his way to the edge of the pool. He picked up a guide staff and examined it with great interest. "Hello, anyone here?" he called out again while looking around.

The door jerked open to slice bright sunshine into the room.

He turned.

Smiling at the stranger, Coco peered into the room. While stepping through the door, her heel caught on the threshold and broke off.

With a squeal, she leaned against the door jamb to survey the damage in disgust. "Oh, poo, I just bought these."

Tom's eyes brightened at the sight of the busty blonde's lush figure. He turned his attention to her broken heel. "Can I help you?" he asked with a cool, gallant voice.

She glanced up at the handsome, tanned, older man. Instantly, she sported her coquettish schoolgirl smile. "I thought I heard someone in here. You wouldn't happen to have an extra pair of Jimmy Choo's on you?"

He smiled. "I'm afraid not. Here. Let me take a look. Perhaps I can fix it for you." He knelt down to slip the pump from her foot.

Her heart skipped a beat when his hand swept over her heel, across her arch, and through her toes. His hands weren't callused like Mike's, or twisted and wrinkled like that mean old Doug O'Conner. He wore a gold ring on his right pinky. She noticed the small gold cross on a chain around her neck.

Just a touch of bling. Sweet.

Tom inspected the shoe, her foot, the delicate curve of her calf, and her slender tight thighs. Trying to collect his thoughts, he cleared his throat and averted his eyes to glance around the room.

Spotting tools on a shelving unit, he retrieved a hammer, placed the heel on the shoe, and tapped it once, during which he smacked his thumb. Wincing, he stuffed the corner of his thumb in his mouth to suck away a bead of blood.

"Are you okay?" Tenderly, she pulled his hand away from his mouth to massage his thumb. Her lips curled while her eyes searched his.

Feeling the electricity in their touch, he didn't pull his hand away. His wince softened. His eyes met hers. "I'll be fine. That should hold long enough for you to return them anyway."

"Thank you." She planted her hand on his shoulder to slip the shoe onto her foot.

He took in her crystal blue eyes, and the splay of blonde hair that had fallen across her soft blushed cheek. She was young, lovely, sultry, and oh-so-entrancing.

"You must be Kate," he said.

"Oh, goodness no, my name is Coco, Coco Beardmore."

Tom's smile turned into a wide grin. "You don't mean, Colette Beardmore? Stan's little girl?"

Her blue eyes twinkled. "Uh-huh. Do you know Daddy?"

"Doesn't everybody? I'm Tom Mason." He took her hand and kissed it gently. "Are you free for lunch, Colette?"

She breathed in. She needed to face Mike in order to release him from any more responsibilities for her horses. *I owe him that. It's the right thing to do after last night.* But she felt quite stimulated by this man who called her Colette. *No one ever called me that. Not Henry, not Daddy, no one ... until now. Perfect.*

"Tom Mason, you're not at all what I expected you to be."

෬ ෮ ෬ ෮

Eric wandered onto the front porch. The steam from the hot coffee whirled above his mug. The morning haze was diminishing to reveal the grandeur of the lush green paddocks and the gentle sway of the oaks. The mist rose off the blue tin roofs of the horse barns.

He noticed the black Porsche parked in front of the equine swimming facility. His eyebrows furrowed when the door opened and Tom Mason emerged with a beautiful blonde on his arm.

He cupped his hand to his mouth. "Tom!"

Tom opened the passenger door of the Porsche for Coco. His attention jerked toward the farmhouse. Whipping his sunglasses from his head, he placed them over his eyes before lifting a hand to wave at Eric.

"Tom, where are you going?" Eric shouted across the way. His calls brought Mike, Shane, and Kate filing out the front door to the porch to catch a glimpse of their father's old friend.

"I'll catch you later, Eric," he shouted back.

"But I thought you wanted to see the horses swim."

Tom slipped into his car next to Coco, "Later, Eric, later."

"Is that Coco in his car?" Kate was rather disturbed by the sight.

Eric scrubbed his chin in concern. "I think so."

The Porsche ripped past the farmhouse.

Spotting Mike, Coco blew a kiss and waved her hand at him like a ballerina making a graceful exit-stage left.

"Ouch, dumped for an older man," Kate quipped in his ear.

"How old is Coco?" Eric asked.

"Thirty-one, maybe thirty-two." Mike shrugged his shoulder while taking a sip of his coffee.

"Yep," Eric confirmed, "that'll work."

"He ain't getting no freaking prize. He'll see." Imitating Doug's gruff voice the day they claimed Coco's horses from his barn, Shane shook a piece of toast at his older brother. With a wink, he moseyed into the house.

The right side of Mike's lip curled. Snorting, he followed his ornery kid brother through the door.

CB   ↄ   CR   ↄ

The old O'Conner farmhouse was more of a shack than a house.

Mike stood at the end of the cracked and heaving sidewalk that led through an over-grown front yard littered with cigarette butts. Chickens pecked at the ground. When he walked through, they scattered while clucking loudly.

He picked his way up to the front porch while climbing over sleeping cats sprawled across the steps. There was an old rocking chair on the porch. Several battered plastic yard chairs and a straw broom leaned against the splintered wooden door frame.

The screen door used to be white, but was now rusty with patches of white paint that had managed to survive to this point. The welcome mat below the door that was so worn that the word *welcome* now read: *We c m*. He couldn't imagine why there would be a welcome mat at all. Doug wasn't exactly hospitable. He was pretty damned sure that the O'Conners didn't do a lot of entertaining.

The sound of snorting horses caught his attention. He peered around the side of the house. Behind a fence made of frayed baler twine strung along old rusted metal posts, several old Thoroughbreds munched on hay. *Doug's got himself a top-notch operation here.*

He rapped on the weather-beaten screen door. A moment later, Margie yanked the equally battered storm door open.

He was surprised that she wasn't as shabbily clad as she usually appeared. Her hair was clean, curled, and pulled back away from her face to accentuate the nose that didn't quite fit. A pair of gold hoops dangled from her earlobes, and she wore pink lip gloss. Her tightly-fitted clean jeans complimented her curves, and her red blouse swept nicely over her perky, ample, breasts.

Confused, she blinked. Mike West was the last person she expected see when she opened the door. *Why is he standing on my porch?*

Mike half-smiled. He wasn't exactly sure what had impelled him to come. "How's dinner sound?"

She didn't respond. Looking at him like he'd just grown another eye, she stood there with the screen door between them.

"I know I should've called first … thought I'd surprise you."

Still nothing. She looked at him.

Footsteps dodging cats on the steps tugged Mike's attention from the catatonic Margie O'Conner, who was keeping the screen door between them like a stone wall.

Scott stepped onto the porch with a smile on his face. He clapped his hand on Mike's shoulder. "Hey there." He peered through the screen to nod at her. "Ready Margie?" He turned to Mike. "We're going dancing. Margie's a great dancer. Hey, how come you're never at the dances?"

Margie opened the screen door to brush past him and make her way to the steps. "We'd better go, Scott. We'll be late,"

"Was there something you needed, Mike?" Scott asked.

He tried to shrug-off the awkward feeling in his gut. "No, nothing at all, thanks." He hitched his chin toward Margie to encourage him to catch up.

Margie wasn't waiting. She marched down the sidewalk with chickens scattering in her wake toward Scott's old pickup truck that was parked behind Mike's shiny, pimped-out dually pickup. She swept a lock of her hair behind her ear. Her lips curled when she reached for the door handle.

Part Three

Progress

Cindy McDonald

~ *Eleven* ~

Three Weeks Later

Jen Fleming was trying like hell to maintain a cool front. Her heart was thrumming in her chest so hard, that she feared Eric could hear it.

There he was ...sipping coffee ...in her office. She hadn't invited him. He simply showed up unexpectedly. He'd never done that before. She always had to "bump" into him on the backside with some lame excuse for her visit.

Progress. This was progress.

She tried to keep up with the conversation, which was difficult because she was too busy watching his deep hazel eyes over her coffee cup. She kept imagining what it would be like to snuggle up on the sofa with this handsome, intelligent gentleman.

Perhaps a crackling fire in the fireplace, a soft comfy fleece throw, hot cocoa, and the Steelers winning by three touchdowns against the Ravens. Nice. Or maybe, the soft glow of candlelight, a fluffy warm comforter over our naked bodies, a smooth red wine, and the Steelers winning by six touchdowns against the Browns. Very nice. Whoa. Slow down, girl. Proceed with caution.

"Well, I'd better get going," she suddenly heard him say.

He stood up and walked toward the door.

She blinked back into the moment. He was leaving. *Damn it.* "Are you sure you don't want anymore coffee, Eric?"

He smiled. "Jen, you've topped me off three times. I'll be bouncing off the walls all day, and I'm going to need all the calm I can pull together. Tom Mason and Coco are coming to the farm today. We've got all the vehicles parked behind Mike's house."

She chuckled. "What happened with Kate's Mustang?"

"Totaled. She's getting a new one tomorrow, I believe."

"I'm glad," Jen said. "She works so hard. Drop by again. I enjoyed our little coffee hour."

"Count on it." With a wink and a smile, he slipped out the door. *Progress.*

CB EO CR EO

Stretching her back, Margie yawned while making her way slowly to the cafeteria to fetch coffee for her father and Scott. She dug for a rubber band in her pocket, pulled her uncombed hair from her drooping shoulders, and then wrapped the band around it. She couldn't understand why she always had to go fetch the coffee. *I'm cleaning the stalls. I'm dumping the buckets. I'm throwing the feed to the horses, and there's Dad sitting on a bale of straw teaching Scott how to chew snuff.*

Poor Scott. He was turning green. His face was contorting in ways she didn't think a face could move. *God bless him.* She wasn't sure he'd be able to drink the coffee anyways. He might be laid-out flat on the floor and praying for death by the time she returned.

She spotted Eric stepping out of the nurse's office when she reached the cafeteria door. Smiling, she held the door open for him. "You feeling okay, Mr. West?"

"Sure, why?"

"Well, you was in Ms. Fleming's office."

"Oh." He stepped through the door. "I was just ... visiting."

"Mmmm, I heard they changed the prices in here. How much is an egg sandwich?"

"I'm not sure. It should be on the board," he said.

"Oh, yeah." She let out a loud snort. "Well, you know me. Forgetting my glasses all the time."

Eric glanced down at the glasses dangling from her faded flannel shirt. "Margie, your glasses are clipped to your shirt pocket."

Margie's hand slowly made its way across her chest to finger the glasses. Her cheeks flushed. Not knowing what to say, she looked away.

"She can't read that sign with those glasses, Eric." Dan Quaide's brawny voice sliced into the moment.

Margie whirled around. "I can so."

"All right then." Dan bristly moved aside. "Read the sign on the door."

Her eyes widened. She worked her jaw, but no words came out.

"Put on the glasses, and read the sign," he insisted again.

Her hands shaking, she lifted the glasses to her nose while glaring at Dan. Tears streamed from under the rims. Embarrassed by Eric's presence, she tore them from her face, ran out the door, down the steps, and toward the stables.

Laughing, Dan yelled after her, "Told ya. Can't read a freaking word."

Eric grabbed him by the shirt. "What the hell's the matter with you? There's no need to humiliate her like that."

"She's a liar."

"You're an ass." With a hard shove against the wall, Eric let go of his shirt.

ೞ   ೮   ೞ   ೮

Margie scrambled through the barn door, plunked down hard on a bale of straw, and buried her face in her hands. Against her forearm, she felt the glasses still clipped to her shirt. She whipped them from the pocket and hurled them at the wall. Horrified at the thought of what Eric West must be thinking, she leaned her head against the wall with her arms folded over her breasts.

That I'm an idiot. That's what he's thinking. Course, all his kids are pretty; and smart; and, well, perfect. That's what they all are. Perfect. I'm just an old ugly idiot.

The outside light sliced into the barn when the door creaked open. "Margie ..." Eric called in a soft tone.

Wiping her wet face, she moaned. "That Dan Quaide. He thinks he's so damned smart. I could 'a read that sign if I wanted to."

He eased down onto the bale next to her and handed her a coffee. "Margie ..."

"He's a real jerk, Mr. West."

"Don't worry about him. All you need is someone to show you how," he told her.

"I can read!" she screeched while looking into his doubt-filled expression. "I'm telling ya, I can."

"Margie, it's time to woman-up. You can't read, but you can do something about it—if you really want to," Eric said with that stern, never say die, tone that he was infamous for.

Biting her lip, she took in a long breath before taking a long sip of coffee. "Eh, it's too late—"

"What're you doing here, West? And what's it too late for?" Scowling, Doug stepped out of the barn office while scratching his backside.

Eric said, "I'm here trying to convince your daughter that it's not too late to learn to read."

Doug's face wrenched. "Are you accusing my Marge of being stupid?" He pointed a twisted finger at Eric and spit a wad of chew to the floor. "She ain't pretty, but she ain't stupid, West." He hobbled toward him.

"Of course not, Doug. She's an intelligent woman, who just can't read. But she can learn. It'll open a whole new world for her."

Doug wasn't buying in. He grimaced through the bulging brown lump in his craggy lip. "What world, West? Where men like your Mike won't give her the time of day? And who's gonna pay for reading lessons? Huh? Not me. I'll tell ya that."

Margie leaned forward on one elbow to cup her chin in her hand. "He's right. I'm thirty-three years old. Reading is something I should'a learned a long time ago. Who'd wanna teach me, anyways?"

Gauging the woman's low regard for herself, Eric hesitated for a moment. She was under her father's thumb and pressed against the floor. He had all the power and he kept her there because she was all he had. Unfortunately for Margie, Doug was all she had.

What will happen when Doug's gone? What will become of a woman possibly in her late forties by then who can't read or write?

It was time to liberate Margie O'Conner from the tyranny that her father had wielded upon her for so many years. "I can teach you ... if you really want to learn."

"Waste of time, West," Doug said. "Time you ain't got."

Shocked, she looked up. "You'd take the time to teach me to read?" she whispered awe struck.

"If you're serious about learning to read and write," Eric said, "I'll teach you. Yes."

Waving his hand in the air, Doug stomped toward his office. "I don't understand the need. She's been fine for thirty-three years. But if you wanna waste your time, West." With one last abrasive look, he turned and slammed the office door.

CB EO CR EO

The water splashed. With a staff clipped to his halter, the horse snorted rhythmically with each stroke while Shane guided him around the pool. Watching the large bay gelding in the water; Mike, Coco, and Tom stood at the far end of the pool. Mike was careful to keep a distance from the pool, the guide poles, and Shane.

"I thought Eric was going to be here," Tom said while intently watching his gelding.

"He must be running a little late," Mike replied. "He'll be here soon, I'm sure."

"Oh, Tom, I'd love to try swimming the horse." She glanced at Mike. "I didn't get a chance last time."

Mike stepped forward, "Well, Coco ..."

"Colette," she insisted with a hitched chin. "My name is Colette."

Tom backed her up all the way. "I don't see the harm, Mike. It looks simple enough. And, if my Colette wants to try, she should be given the chance."

Okay, I get it. Tom's sleeping with her. Tom, the older man, is getting to see Coco—Colette—naked. He wants to keep her happy so he can continue to see her naked. I get that, too.

Mike was bracing for a dive into the dirty horse water to pull Colette out after she tripped, or stumbled, or slipped, or some kind of calamity occurred that caused her to take a flying leap into the pool. Even though that wasn't the case last time, he was having no problem picturing it this time.

He turned to Shane, whose eyes were as big as cue balls. "Give her the staff," he said.

With a shrug, Shane handed Colette the pole and backed out of range.

With his hands clasped behind his back, Tom was grinning like an idiot while she guided the horse around the perimeter of the pool. "You look like a pro, sugar plum."

Urgh, Mike's stomach turned.

Shane leaned in close to his ear. "Sugar plum," he playfully mimicked for his older brother's benefit. He could be as irritating as poison ivy in the groin. "Oh yeah, she's sweet as sugar. I can attest to that."

"Shut up," Mike said under his breath and through clenched teeth.

"It's easy, Tom-Tom, give it a try." Colette waved him toward her.

Wanting to come-off as sporting, he hurried to her side to take the guide pole and walk alongside the huffing and puffing horse.

She clapped her hands in delight.

Smiling, Tom looked over his shoulder at her while approaching the narrow bridge that lay over the entrance ramp of the pool, which was where he caught his toe on the lip. Slipping on the wet surface, with arms flailing in the air; he stumbled and fell on top of the horse to straddle it like a jockey.

"Tom-Tom!" Colette shrieked.

"Shiiiit," Mike muttered. He was impressed with the landing.

In the water, the gelding thrashed and snorted in a panic.

Coco ran alongside the pool while grabbing for Tom's arms. Yelping, he reached out to her. "Mike, help!" she cried.

Mike leaned in close to Shane. "I'm really not sure what she wants me to do." Calmly, he held his position.

"Tom-Tom looks like a pro to me." Shane folded his arms over his chest.

Frantic, Colette managed to grasp Tom's hands and yank him toward her. She fell backward to the floor with Tom landing on top of her.

Dripping, Tom looked into her concerned eyes and burst into laughter. "Exhilarating! I've never had so much fun!"

Mike and Shane's mouths dropped. Their eyes popped.

Tom pulled Colette to her feet and kissed her hard. "That's it. From now on we'll ride the horses while they swim. We'll all exercise together."

Christ, this guy can't be for real. At a sprint, Mike was now closing the distance between him and them. "You can't do that."

"Why not? I just did!" Tom exclaimed joyfully.

"That was an accident. It could have turned out very badly—" Mike began.

Tom wrapped his wet arm around his shoulders to tug him to a more private space. "Mike, Mike, you need to chill-out," he said in a jovial voice. He dropped his voice to a whisper, "I know you and Colette had a thing, a little affair. I understand. Forgive and forget. That's what I always say. No hard feelings, man. This will give Colette and me a chance to bond with the horses—Make them feel part of a family. You understand, don't you?"

Forgive and forget? What should I be forgiving? The fact that me and Coco never had a "thing"? Or maybe I should be forgetting that I never saw Coco naked, and we never got to have a "thing".

"You're freaking nuts," he said.

"No, Colette's dog is nuts." Tom laughed.

Ahhh, Mike thought, *so Tom's experienced Booger's little doggy libido. Wonder if Coco's cooked for him in that little black do-things-to-me dress, or worse yet ... naked?*

He clapped his hand on Mike's shoulder. "You'll see. We'll put my horse and Colette's on the program immediately. It'll all work out."

"Coco's horses?" Mike was hitting the panic button. "Those horses are *un-race-able.* They need a new vocation."

But Tom was on an unreachable plain, in a zone, in love with a fantasy, and a beautiful blonde. Her Cocker Spaniel? Maybe not so much.

Eric and Kate walked through the door. "Tom, what happened?" Eric asked in a high-pitched tone of concern while taking in Tom's soaked-to-the-skin condition.

Grabbing Colette by the hand, Tom smiled at his old friend. "The time of my life, Eric, the time of my life. Gotta go, we'll be back in a few days." He turned to Mike. "Have the horses ready." He and Colette trotted gleefully out the door.

"Make sure they get out of the driveway safely." Eric pushed Mike toward the door before turning to Shane, who was leading the exhausted huffing horse out of the pool while opening a soda. "What's going on?"

Shane said, "New training procedures. Where've you been?"

Eric glanced down at his watch. "Doesn't matter, I've got to get cleaned up a bit."

"Where are you going?" Kate asked.

"I have to see someone."

She grew a smug grin. Through narrowed eyes, she looked at him suspiciously. "Jen Fleming?"

"No, Margie O'Conner."

Shane choked on his soda. "Mangy Margie?"

Eric glared at his younger son. "What the hell is wrong with you? Why would you call her that?"

"Have you *met* her?" he retorted. His father continued to glare at him, which prompted him to back down and clear his throat. "What are you going to see her for?"

"I'm teaching her to read." He walked out the door.

Kate's lips parted in surprise. "I didn't know Margie couldn't read." She sighed. "That's kinda sweet. Dad's teaching her to read."

"Oooh, Mike's not gonna like this," Shane said.

"Why not?"

"Margie's always had a thing for Mike. He's gonna have a stroke if Dad brings her around."

"She's a little rough around the edges is all—kind of like Audrey Hepburn."

"Who?" he asked.

"Audrey Hepburn," she explained. "She was ignorant and dirty until Rex Harrison came along and taught her to read, and write, and speak properly."

Totally lost, he said, "I don't know her. This happened at our track?"

Kate rolled her eyes. A little light in the attic came on. "Does Mike have a date for the benefit dance next month?"

To raise funds for hospital and household expenses, twice a year the Jockey's Association put on a benefit dance for jockey's that had been seriously injured while racing.

Shane shrugged.

There was the sudden gleam in Kate's blue meddling eyes. "Maybe Dad is trying to prep Margie for the benefit dance." She was no longer gleaming, she was beaming at the Eliza Doolittle notion.

Shane wasn't getting it, but he was sure of one thing. "Mike's screwed," he said with a wince.

~ *Twelve* ~

The evening shadows were starting to filter down from the old maple tree's branches that drooped over the rickety wooden gate at the end of the cracked sidewalk. The untrimmed trees hanging over the house created an ominous setting.

After parking his black Denali, Eric measured the battered farmhouse, the old Thoroughbreds behind the baler twine fence, and the falling-down barn.

Doug didn't make a bad living as a trainer. In fact, he had a decent racing record. Several times a year, his name appeared on the top ten trainers list at Keystone Downs. But Doug was a hard man. He trained hard; he spoke hard; and, from the looks of his farm, he lived hard, as well.

Too bad for Margie.

Eric scooted the little gate open to trace the arced impression the gate had engraved in the ground beneath it. Cackling a warning that someone was approaching, chickens scattered.

A cat screeched frantically when Eric stepped on its tail on his way up the steps. When he jumped back, the cats scampered in different directions beneath his feet to flee the intruder.

A single sixty-watt bulb hung from a wire near the weather-scarred screen door. He rapped on the door, which vibrated under his fist. *Click,*

click, click. Several latches on the other side turned, twisted, and popped before the door finally jerked open.

Margie peeked at him from inside. "Hi, Mr. West, come in." She swung the door open.

Her hair was pulled back into a neat ponytail. Silver hoops dangled from her ears. Her jeans were fresh and fitted, and her blue blouse was pristine.

The living room was surprisingly neat and clean, in spite of its worn-out condition. The wood floor was in desperate need of refinishing. Old and in disrepair, the furniture consisted of a dull green floral couch and a gold striped over-stuffed chair that didn't match. A brown brick fireplace took up the far wall. The mantel was filled with photographs of Thoroughbreds in old tattered wood frames. The laminate early-American coffee tables held ashtrays and pitted brass lamps that didn't match anything else in the room. Well-used spittoons rested next to the couch and chair.

Margie led him into a tiny kitchen with metal cabinets, scuffed linoleum, and a wooden table with three wobbly puritan-style chairs. A brass spittoon rested next to the leg of a chair with a crushed, frayed, blue pillow on the seat—Doug's chair, no doubt.

"Have a seat, Mr. West." Margie nervously fingered an earring.

The left side of his mouth curved. "Margie, if we're going to be spending time together, I think you should call me Eric."

The suggestion urged a timid smile. "All right, I'll try to call you Eric, Mr. West."

He chuckled. "Good. How did practice go?"

Her eyes brightened. The timid smile grew to a full-blown grin. "Good." She hurried to the counter to retrieve a clipboard. Oozing with pride, she presented it to Eric. She clasped her hands to her chest and watched attentively while he looked over her work.

He smiled again at the woman before him. "Very good indeed. I'm glad I sent Pedro over with this clipboard this afternoon." He sat at the table. "Can you write your name for me?" He ripped away several used-up, scribbled-on papers to expose a fresh sheet. "Without looking at the practice sheet?"

Sinking into the chair next to him, Margie met his confident gaze with enthusiasm. "I think so." She picked up the pencil.

She uncovered a dish of cookies on the table and slid it toward him. "I hope you like oatmeal-raisin cookies. I baked them myself."

"They're my favorite." He took a bite of one of the cookies and pressed his eyes closed to savor the flavor. "Mmmm, reminds me of the cookies my wife used to make."

The pride-filled grin returned to her gaunt, unattractive face, and her lovely dark eyes filled with satisfaction.

She took the pencil and slowly, painstakingly, formed each letter of her name. He could see the absolute concentration on her face. His heart felt heavy for this woman, who had been robbed of the basic right to learn to read and write. It wasn't hard to recognize her strong constitution to seize what had eluded her all these years. Yet, she did not hold any bitterness toward her father for the thievery. In fact, it seemed she loved him, and was beholden to him for the life she had.

Finally, she held the clipboard up for him. Her eyes were moist with accomplishment.

Progress, this was indeed progress.

"Very good, Margie. No more fake glasses, and soon, no more asking anyone to read for you. Now, let's get started."

03 80 03 80

With a can of Iron City in his fist, Doug leaned against the doorway of his bedroom while watching a man he had no use for teaching his daughter something he had never bothered with. Wishing Eric would mind his own damned business, he glowered at him. *What's in it for him? Hell, I would never spend time sitting around a table with someone I barely knew if there weren't no benefits to it. What's his angle? There's gotta be one.*

Taking another swig of Iron City, he retreated into his bedroom and closed the door.

03 80 03 80

Ahhh, Thursday morning! Eric breathed in the smell of the sweet hay piled in the barn's aisle while leading his old grey Quarter Horse gelding from his stall. Ike was saddled and bridled, and ready for some outrider action.

Thursday was the day that the Wests did not go to Keystone Downs. They worked the horses at their own training track at the farm. Eric and Ike; or Bert and Ernie, as Kate fondly referred to them; would position themselves at the far end of the training track, and wait for an exercise rider to loose control of a mount. Ike's ears would perk when Eric booted him in the sides, tossed him the reins, and ran down the out-of-control Thoroughbred until they were alongside the horse, where Eric could reach over, grab the reins, and slow him to a stop.

Oh, yeah, those were the exciting Thursday mornings. Every Thursday? No, some Thursday mornings, Eric and Ike would sit at their post, sip coffee, take in the view, and never be summoned. Those were the boring Thursdays. At least they were out in the fresh air to enjoy the view.

Eric checked the girth one more time.

"Dad," Mike bellowed from the end of the barn.

Eric turned to see his elder son jogging toward him. He didn't look happy.

Mike's head was spinning. Shane couldn't wait to spill the news that their father was tutoring Margie, and she would more-than-likely be visiting the farm, often. Shane's eyes twinkled with satanic joy when he shared the information with his big brother.

Mike shrugged it off at first, but after giving it more thought and letting it marinate a big twinge of panic hit him in the gut.

He conferred with Kate, a more reliable source, about the rumor. Yet, she rambled on and on about some girl named Eliza. *Never heard of her, maybe she's a new jockey at the track. Kate isn't making any sense at all. She seems to have stars in her eyes. What the hell is wrong with her today? Women.*

Eric swung a leg over Ike and fidgeted in the saddle for a comfortable position.

"Dad, what's going on?" he asked his father breathlessly.

"Today's Thursday. I'm the outrider."

"Shane said you were at Margie O'Conner's house last night."
If Shane is screwing with me, I'm gonna have to kick his ass.

Eric adjusted his reins. "Yep."

"Hey, look Dad—"

Eric settled into the saddle. "Calm down, Mike. I'm just teaching her to read. I haven't made some covert deal with Doug to marry you off to his daughter." He nudged Ike forward toward the barn door. "I'm not sure he'd have it anyway," he added under his breath.

"Well, how long is that gonna take?" Mike called after him.

Eric tossed his hands in the air. He and Ike exited the barn.

CB 80 CR 80

Two Weeks Later

A cool breeze blew through the O'Conner kitchen while Margie and Eric worked through an old reader that he had found in the attic. It was outdated, and the pages were brown; but it would serve the purpose at hand, Eric figured.

As always during their tutoring sessions, there was a platter of homemade cookies and dessert breads on the table. Eric was amazed at the array of goodies she would prepare: cookies, apple pie, peach pie, cherry pie, pumpkin bread, and banana bread. It was truly impressive how this woman could bake so many things without being able to read or write down a recipe.

Margie wanted to show her sincere gratitude for his time and patience. Baking was the only thing she thought she excelled at. Motivated and smart, she was proving herself wrong.

She was improving in the brush and comb department, as well. Desiring a different look to go with her new self, she bought beauty magazines to learn new hairstyles. She was considering trying some make-up techniques, as well.

Each time Eric arrived, her hair was neatly pulled-back in a pony-tail, or a tight bun. Sometimes, she would draw up the sides and allow the back to cascade over her shoulders. She was getting damned good at using a curling iron.

"See Dick run. Run Dick run. H ... he ... he ..." Margie stammered.

"Hear," Eric helped out. When she looked puzzled, he explained, "Not like come here, but rather hear … like with your ears."

"Oooh. Hear Spot b-b-bark." She smiled. "Bark, Spot, bark." She looked at him for confirmation and praise.

He didn't disappoint her. "Very good. You've come a long way in only two short weeks."

"Oh, I know, and ya know what? I'm gonna learn how to use a computer and everything." She glanced around the kitchen. "I wanna show you something."

She retrieved a book from a drawer and handed it to him while keeping watch for her father. Eric examined the Harlequin Romance book that was dated from the 1980s.

"I found a whole box of these in the basement," she told him in low voice. "I got them hid under my bed. They were my mother's. I used to look at the covers every night before I went to sleep. It's all I have of her."

Once again, Eric's heart agonized for her; but her eyes were bright, hopeful, and determined.

She told him, "When I've learned to read good, and learn how to use a computer, I'm gonna look for her. Did you know her, Mr. West … Eric?"

Regret filled his eyes. He sucked in his lips. "No, Margie. I never met your mother."

"I'm gonna meet her," she said softly while staring with longing at the book. "And I'll have you to thank."

He tried to change the mood up a notch. "Ahhh, it's worth it. Look at all the great treats I get."

With a smile, she tilted her head and lifted a shoulder. "It's the least I can do."

"I'm going to get fat, ya know."

"You? Never. Pleasantly plump, maybe." She let out a laugh, and fell silent while gazing at his handsome face. She could see where Mike got his mysterious, daunting hazel eyes.

"Well, that's enough for tonight. I better get home." He pushed away from the table.

She walked him to the door. "Make sure you tell Mike I said hey."

"I will." Eric carefully stepped over a sleeping cat as she closed the screen door behind him.

"She's kinda young for you, eh West?"

Doug's miserable voice crept from the shadows at the edge of the porch to bring Eric to a halt. He turned. Wrapped in an afghan, Doug rocked back and forth on an old rocker while tapping an empty beer can on its arm.

"What the hell are you so afraid of, Doug? That Margie will realize there's a world out there beyond Keystone Downs—and *you?*" Eric remarked in a clipped tone.

"She's a good girl, my Marge." He slurred his words.

"She's not a girl. She's a woman. And you've treated her like your personal servant for as long as I can remember."

Doug attempted to stand, but the rocker got the best of him to force him back into the seat. "You get outta here, West. And I don't want you around here no more, ya hear me?"

"I hear ya, Doug. Too bad you can't hear yourself." Scattering the chickens, Eric made his way down the lopsided cracked sidewalk.

"Margie, get me a beer!" the old bugger bellowed for Eric's benefit.

She watched through the screen. Eric hesitated before continuing through the gate.

"Margie!"

Jolted back to the moment, she blinked hard before darting into the kitchen to retrieve Doug's beer.

C3 80 C3 80

On the long way home, Eric found himself driving slower than usual.

In the silence of the night ride, with the windows down and radio off; he was immersed in thought. He'd been thinking a lot lately … about Jen Fleming. She was a very attractive woman. The way her short brunette hair curled around her heart-shaped chin. Her big, brown eyes were kind, compassionate. *Hey, they're pretty damned sexy, too.*

She was always stopping by the stables with really lame "professional" reasons. Like, he needed to sign an insurance form that he'd signed two days before; or she needed the name of a hired stable hand that didn't exist. He knew. He never let on, but he knew, and he liked it.

It's time to stop liking it, and do something about it, damn it. It's been ten years since Barbara died. Ten years, Eric. It's time to move on with your life. Who knows? Jen Fleming may be just the woman to move on with. Okay, time to end the cat and mouse game. Time to make a move.

Margie was making great progress. It was time to make some progress of his own. Smiling to himself, he steered the Denali through the stone entrance of Westwood.

ભ ૭૦ ભ ૭૦

The mid-morning sun glimmered through the maple trees that lined the racetrack at Keystone Downs. The morning workouts were over, and the John Deeres raked the dirt surface to prepare it for the evening races.

At a picnic table under a huge maple, Margie practiced writing her name over and over again. She worked each letter with meticulous attention. The next time the UPS man asked for her signature on a package, she wanted her signature to be perfect.

Her father had forbidden Eric to come to the house, so he was now tutoring her at the track after morning workouts.

People noticed them at the picnic table. Some would call-out and wave to them. Suspicious of the pair, some would stop and watch before continuing on their way. Margie and Eric paid them no mind. They had important business to tend to, and she felt so lucky to be important enough for Eric West to spend time with her.

Margie thought it was imperative to look as nice as possible for her sessions. It helped with her learning. She made sure her hair was neat and clean. Today, she wore it braided and cascading over her shoulder while she worked.

She had bought some Cover Girl eye shadow, which she brushed a little green over her lids. After struggling with the mascara, she wiped it off and decided to learn how to apply that another day.

She had changed from her barn clothes to fresh jeans and a green shirt before going to the picnic table. She looked good in green … considering. All in all, it was a poor attempt at perfection. She would never be as beautiful as Kate or Ava West. Christ, all the Wests seemed to be perfect. Perfect complexions, hair, eyes, and they all had bodies like workout gurus.

I'll never be beautiful like them, but I'll no longer be an idiot. I will be able to read, and write, and sign my name neatly when the UPS man comes. Perfect might be out of reach. Average is the best I'll most likely ever be.

Glancing at the plate of snicker-doodles she'd baked for today's lesson, another thought occurred to her. *Those women are pretty, but they probably don't bake half as well as I can. Lord knows, Eric sure does love my baking. He's even compared it to his wife's.*

Take that pretty girls.

She had just finished the letter *E* in her first name, when a shadow hovered over her. Thinking it was Eric arriving, she turned to greet him with a smile, only to find Dan Quaide with a smirk on his coarse face.

Dan made an effort at pleasant. "Hey, Margie, whatcha doing?"

She turned away to concentrate on the letter *O*. "I'm busy, Dan," she replied curtly.

"With what?"

Annoyed, she let out a sigh. "Practicing my—It's none of your damned business." She was hoping to hear his footsteps retreating through the grass so that she could finish her last name.

He continued watching over her shoulder. "What're you and ol' Eric up to under this tree?" he asked with a snort.

She whipped around. Her eyebrows furrowed. "He's teaching me to read and write."

He snorted louder and harder. "Is that what they're calling it nowadays?"

"Shut-up."

Refusing to leave it at that, he leaned down on the table. His tone was mean and teasing. "Is he taking you to the dance next week?"

She slid across the seat. "Why would he?"

Dan burst into a laugh. "You're right. He'd have to really lower his standards to show up with you." He snatched her clipboard from the table. "Hey, lemme see what you're writing."

Margie's breath caught. She grabbed for it, but Dan backed away too fast. Grappling for the clipboard, she jumped from her seat. Merrily, he danced in circles while holding it over her head and watching her struggle to claim it.

"Give it to me, Dan!" Tears formed in her eyes.

"I just wanna see what he's really been teaching you at night."

She begged, "Please, Dan. I got work to do."

"Just let me—"

"Dan!" Eric's bellow ripped through the struggle.

Dan froze. Wearing a cock-eyed smile, he turned. "Hey, Eric, how's things?"

Eric leaned against the tree with his arms crossed over his chest. "What are you? Twelve?"

Dan suddenly became aware of the crowd that had gathered to stare at him like he wasn't wearing pants.

"Give her the clipboard," Eric strongly advised.

Margie seized the clipboard from the brawny man and folded it into her chest. She lowered her head to hide her flushed face.

Dan held his hands up. "Hey, I don't want to get in the way of progress."

Eric's tight gaze never wavered. He nodded. "Wise decision."

Dan looked around at the crowd. Stuffing his hands into his pockets, he whistled when he walked away.

Eric pushed away from the tree to take a seat next to Margie at the picnic table.

CB ƎO CR ꝏ

Amongst the dispersing crowd, Kate watched her father getting down to the business of teaching the young woman. Biting her lip, she wore a worrisome expression. The murmurs in the group were filled with innuendos of a surprising affair between the older, wealthy, horseman and the younger not-so-attractive woman. No one saw what her father was doing for this woman. No one really cared what was really going on. Oh no, the dirty, little rumors were much more entertaining.

Ava strolled up behind her to draw close to her ear. "He's been spending a lot of time with her, hasn't he?" she chirped. "She doesn't seem like his type, but you never know, do you?"

~ Thirteen ~

Tom was pumped. Anticipating a vigorous swim with his Thoroughbred, Ivan; he waited next to the pool. Stuffed into a red Speedo, he consciously sucked in his tanned abs. The gold chain and cross shined against his dark curly chest hairs sparsely spread over his torso and down his abs to circle his navel.

Unable to look at him, Mike kept his eyes focused on the floor, on the horse, on the windows, on the pool, on anything at all in order to not to have to look at the bulge covered only by a thin piece of spandex between Tom's legs.

Gee-zuz, man, is he for real?

"Give me a leg up, Mike. Lead us into the pool," Tom said with the enthusiasm of an over-zealous child at an amusement park.

Mike's eyes bugged. The last thing he wanted to do was grab this man's leg and have his "boys" directly in his face. *No way in hell.* Desperately, he glanced around the large room.

Where the hell is Coco? He had called her the night before to try like hell to talk some sense into that blonde brain of hers before Tom took the big splash. *I hope she heard what I was telling her.* All he got back from the conversation was, "Uh, huh," "Mmmm," and a few "Okay's." Maybe he had called her at a bad time, or a good one … it was all in the perception.

Here Tom was, practically in his birthday suit, ready to take the plunge. *Obviously, Coco wasn't able to talk him out of this crazy idea. Maybe she's as crazy as he is.*

"Mike ..." With his leg hoisted, Tom stood close while poised for him to give a lift onto the horse's back. "What are you waiting for?"

"Divine intervention," Mike murmured under his breath.

"Tom-Tom." Coco's voice rang out from across the room.

Mike turned.

There she was—in all her glory—wearing a hot pink, string bikini. Her perky, round breasts bounced gently when she strutted toward him in a pair of pink stilettos. Her shapely hips eased down into her long, lean legs. No ballerina could be more beautiful while gliding across the room toward the edge of the pool to look down into the water.

He closed his eyes. *Well, she's almost naked.* He couldn't think about that. Coco was about to do a really big no-no. He had to put a stop to this dangerous game they were adamant on playing.

He heard her voice again. "Tom." This time her voice was stern, almost scolding. Mike opened his eyes to a sight he never thought he'd witness. She was peering into the horse water, with her hands firmly on her gorgeous hips and an uncompromising look on her face.

Sexy.

Tom dropped his foot to the floor. *Thank God.* He was peering over the horse at her.

"Tom, I've had second thoughts," she stated decisively. Her nose wrinkled at the sight of the less than crystal clear water.

Oh yeah, she doesn't like what she's looking at. She is definitely in control mode. Very sexy.

"I think Mike knows best. We should leave the swimming to him."

Mike exhaled. "Thanks, Coco."

"It's Colette," she corrected him in a firm voice.

Ballerina sexy.

Tom's lower lip drooped far and low. "Do you mean, let Mike ride while the horse swims?"

Terrified that in fact that was exactly what the sexy little blonde meant, Mike's entire body stiffened. He braced for yet another Coco calamity. Only this time it would be at his expense. *Aren't they all?*

"No, Tom, I mean leave the training to the professional." Her eyes scanned the water again before landing on the gentlemanly cowboy. She tossed him a resolute look. "Isn't that best, Mike?" She wasn't begging for his confirmation, she was damn well demanding it.

"It is ... Colette," he assured her with a soft, half-smile.

She returned his smile with her lips and her eyes. She made her way to him, brushed a stray strand away from his eyes, and kissed his cheek tenderly to urge another smile out of him.

"Thank you, Mike." She squared her shoulders. "I wanted you to know that I've made arrangements for my horses to be shipped to a Thoroughbred placement program." She squeezed his arm. "I feel really badly about what happened to Sebastian. I don't want Charlatan to hurt anyone ever again, but I want him to have a good home."

"Another good decision, Colette." Relief filled Mike's voice.

"Thanks again, my gentlemanly cowboy." With that, she took Tom by the hand to lead him, and his Speedo, from the swimming facility.

Mike held on to his smile. He was amazed how far Coco—Colette had come in only a few, short weeks. A strange metamorphosis had taken place. From the train wreck to the cool-headed, rational—and yes—in control—individual in the relationship. Still, he wished one of those damned strings would come undone and that bikini come tumbling down. *Seeing Coco naked just plain wasn't meant to be. Damn it.*

Forgiving just became a whole lot easier. Forget? No, not really. I don't want to forget Coco—Not the calamities she caused. Not her twinkling crystal blue eyes. She is beautiful and kind. She never used her beauty to manipulate or hurt anyone. No, forgetting Miss Colette Beardmore is not a viable option.

Progress.

ଊ ଓ ଏ ଓ

Today was the day. Eric wasn't going to put it off any longer. He was going to march into Jen Fleming's office and take the first step toward a future. He was sure she was feeling the same way—pretty sure, anyway.

Morning workouts were finished. Reviewing nouns and pronouns, he'd spent an hour with Margie. Now, he stood outside Jen's office door with his hand on the knob. He sucked in a deep breath, and tapped on the door while he pressed through.

Nobody.

The office was quiet and still.

Jen's metal desk rested along the wall with two stacked baskets filled with neatly piled papers on the right corner. Several framed pictures of her son, Brandon, took up the desk's left corner.

Eric picked up one of the pictures. He'd never met Brandon. The young man, whose last name was Marshall, rarely came back to Lanzville. *Jen must have been married before, and took back her maiden name after a divorce.* She never spoke of it, and he didn't feel that he should pry. *She'll tell me when she's ready.*

"Looking for me?" Jen slipped through the door.

Startled, Eric replaced the picture on the desk. "Yes, I just dripped by ... I mean, I just *dropped* by."

She tossed him a befuddled look. She had never seen him unraveled. "Is something wrong, Eric?"

"No, no, I ..." The words were catching in his throat.

This used to be easier—back when I was young, and romancing my wife. Now? It seems awkward, and ridiculous. Deciding to take the plunge, Eric shook his head and took a deep breath. He squared his shoulders and looked her in the eye. "I came to see if you were available for the benefit dance next week."

At last. She gazed into his anxiety-filled expression that was anticipating her response. *How cute is this? He's like a nervous teenager— adorable. Should I make him wait for my answer? I don't want to seem too eager. But he looks so incredibly handsome standing there all vulnerable and anxious.* She had never seen the imposing man like this before. It made her want to push him against the wall, smash her lips against his, and see where things went after that.

She held her poker-face. "Are you asking me to go with you?" She didn't want to jump at the proposal, and she certainly didn't want any misunderstandings at this point in the game.

Good God, didn't I make that clear? He was feeling really rusty at this stuff. "Yes, if you'd like to go with me," he admitted coyly.

Her plan was waning. She'd waited so long for this man to want to be with her, and she so wanted to be with him. *To hell with looking too eager.* "Of course, I'll go with you." She was quite pleased with herself that she didn't seem overly enthusiastic, or at least she hoped.

Eric smiled in relief. Looking into those big, brown, damned sexy eyes, he couldn't help himself anymore. Gently, he took her by the shoulders, drew her close, and pressed his lips tenderly to hers.

She wrapped her arms around his waist and kissed him back just as gently, just as wanting, and just as relieved. *At last, at last, he's come to me. I've waited for so long, dropped so many hints, and now here he is, kissing me. I don't want to let go. Ahhh, sweet, sweet, progress.*

Out of nowhere, there was another presence in the room—clearing her throat. Eric and Jen jerked away from their embrace and met Ava's haughty smirk.

Jen brushed a brunette lock from her face. "Ava, what can I do for you?" She pounced into the all-business track nurse mode.

"Could you take a look at this cut? I think it's infected, and I'm really tired of having Doc Spears look at things for me." She held out her bandaged right hand.

Eric cleared his throat. "I'd better be going. I'll see you later?"

Jen's breath caught. *What? Is he kidding?* "Oh, yes, I'll definitely see you later, Eric."

Ava waited for the door to click closed before she seized the moment. "Good for you, Jennifer Fleming. When were you going to share the good news?"

Jen lifted a shoulder while pulling a bottle of antiseptic solution and gauze pads from a cabinet. "There's nothing to share ... yet." She was trying to control her excitement; but, the way her head was swimming, she feared it was a losing battle.

Ava's lips curled in deviant delight. "Mmmm, I'm totally thrilled. You know, he's been getting way too cozy with the O'Conner girl. I'm so glad he's not one of those older men who always fall for younger women."

Jen hesitated. *Eric is much too level-headed for that. Right?*

The barn was rocking. Alan Jackson and Jimmy Buffett were singing about the possibility of it being five o'clock somewhere.

Perusing *Glamour Magazine*, Margie studied the season's new eye colors while taking a break on a bale of straw. She'd never enjoyed time at the barn as much as she was at that moment. Upbeat, modern country music was blasting from the old radio. Actually, she was surprised that the radio hadn't exploded. It had never been on any station except Old Country Gold.

Her foot was tapping, her head was bobbing, and her eyes were wide with the prospect of a new her. *Maybe I can't be as beautiful as Kate, or Ava, or even Coco—maybe perfection is out of my reach, but I sure can take it up a notch. I'll show Mike West what he's been missing out on all these years. Thanks to his own father.* She giggled to herself at the idea. *Sooner or later, he'll want to do more than have dinner.*

"What the hell is going on in here?" Doug's bellow sliced into her private party. He ripped the radio's cord from the wall to abruptly silence Jackson and Buffett.

Margie never glanced up from her magazine.

Infuriated by her dismissal, he marched to her and snatched the magazine from her hands. Now he had her attention. "What's the matter with you? Reading this trash, listening to that garbage. Who told you to change the station on my radio?" He was flabbergasted by her shocking mutiny. He didn't see it coming. He couldn't imagine the day his Marge would defy him. *Eric West, that's who's responsible for this. Damn him to hell.*

Hurling the magazine into the trash can, he glowered at her as if she were a total stranger caught stealing money in his barn. If she were a young girl, he'd give her a good thrashing. But, Eric West was right about one thing. *She's a woman.*

Shit! What was I thinking? The night Eric stood on my porch telling me how to handle my daughter—I should have told him then and there not only to not come back but never to see Marge again. But Marge wanted it so bad, and she never really asked for anything, so I let it go on. It's gone too far. Now what?

Margie wasn't having it. She grabbed the magazine from the trash and plugged the radio into the wall. "I'll turn it down so it won't bother you as much, but I'm listening to this music, Dad. I'm thirty-three, and I've listened to Johnny Cash for the last time." She tucked the magazine under her arm. "I'm going to the cafeteria for some lunch. You want anything?"

She waited for a response. When none came, she pushed through the barn door with Gretchen Wilson screaming "Hell ya!" from the old, dusty radio.

On her way out the door, she bumped into Scott so hard that she almost knocked him to the ground. "Oh," she yelped.

"Everyone's always in such a big hurry around here." He held on to her arms. "Will you be ready by seven to go dancing tonight?"

Searching for words, Margie dropped her gaze to the ground. "I'm sorry, Scott. I can't go with you tonight. I'm studying with Eric at his house." Slowly she lifted her eyes to meet his.

He tried to hide the disappointment and the hurt, but he was failing miserably. "Oh ... no problem." He forced a fake smile of poise. "I'll catch ya another time, Marge." He squeezed her arms gently. Dropping his chin, he pressed through the barn door.

CB ED CR ED

Doug dropped down on the bale of straw. He'd lost his Marge. She was a goner, and he wasn't quite sure what he was going do about it. He spit the last wad of tobacco to the ground.

Shuffling down the barn aisle with his shoulders drooped, Scott paused to assess the old codger feeling the same sense of loss he felt. He had seen the changes in Margie in these last weeks. Some might call it progress. To him, it seemed like she was slipping away from everything she knew and loved. He sank onto the bale next to Doug.

"I don't like it, Scott. I tell ya, I don't like it. I see the way she looks at that old man. It ain't healthy. It ain't normal." Doug bawled while stuffing a fresh gob of snuff in his lip. He offered some to Scott.

His lip curling, Scott winced and backed away. "I don't think you gotta worry about ol' Eric West. I think he's got himself a girlfriend." Doug's eyes brightened while he continued, "I see him coming and going from the nurse's office all the time. He don't strike me as being sick."

"So, you think the reading lessons might be coming to a end?"

Scott wanted the old Margie back in the worst sort of way. She hadn't been going to the dances. She was too busy studying her reading or writing, or whatever the hell she was studying. She was spending her time in some La-La Land fantasy that he couldn't comprehend.

What he could understand was how he felt about her. Most men found her unattractive. Not him. She had the most beautiful eyes he'd ever seen. He fell in love with those eyes the first time he'd looked into them. They were filled with kindness and compassion. He was most certain that there was a passion inside that woman that was waiting to claw its way to the surface.

Enough was enough. It was time for a reality check. It was time to put some distance between her and the so-called "beautiful people" that were trying to pervert her. No time like the present, and even less to waste.

He reached down and scooped a stone from the floor. "They'll be ending real soon," he told Doug.

CB EO CB EO

Margie leaned against the counter while waiting for her turn to order.

As it always was after morning workouts, the cafeteria was packed. At a corner table, old weathered retired jockeys smoked cigarettes and rubbed their arthritic knees while watching several exercise boys playing a game of pool near the door. The jukebox moaned an old Johnny Cash tune in the background.

Seriously? Margie rolled her eyes at yet another old country tune. Halfway through the disgusted roll they fell upon Eric and Jen huddled over their cups of coffee at a corner table. *Hmmm.*

"Hey, Margie, how've you been?" Ava's voice took her by surprise.

"Fine. Yourself?" She kept her eyes locked on Eric and Jen while wondering what the relationship might be.

Noting Margie's interest, Ava was more than happy to bring her up-to-date. "Oh, I see Jen Fleming's trying to get her hooks into Eric West." Margie's eyes rotated toward her. Ava leaned in a little closer to lay it on thick. "Ya know, I was talking with Michael, and he was telling me how much Eric adores you."

Margie's chin drew back in disbelief. "He did?"

"Don't be so surprised. Men are attracted to younger women—especially those who need their help. It makes them feel desirable."

Margie's forehead wrinkled in doubt. "I don't know ..."

"Absolutely, Eric has already proven it to you. Think about it ... the way he defended you against Dan Quaide the other day. Something tells me it's not the first time he's come to your defense." Affirming, assuring, and convincing, she kept her green eyes firmly on hers.

Margie swiped a lock of hair behind her ear. Her mind took her back to the evening on the porch when her father told Eric never to come back to the farm. He could have called it quits on the reading lessons, but he didn't. He'd made arrangements to meet her elsewhere. Ava definitely had a point. Eric was older, more settled, and less impressed by beautiful woman.

Hmmm. She was mystified by this new concept. *Why didn't I see it before? Hey, it is possible.* She looked through narrowed eyes while cocking her chin. "Are you serious?"

Ava smiled confidently. "As a heart attack. It makes them feel important ... *heroic.*" She hitched her chin toward the cozy corner table. "But I'd watch ol' Jen Fleming if I were you. She's been trying to get a grip on Eric since ... well, since forever."

Margie measured Jen Fleming. She was lovely, not as beautiful as Ava, but lovely none-the-less. "I can't compete with that."

Ava took in Margie's homely face, mousey brown hair. Her fashion sense was a toss-up between bad, very bad, and What-the-hell-are-you-wearing? *She'll be a challenge.* Ava loved a challenge. Most of all, she loved to make bullets.

"There's more than one way to skin a cat, sweetie. Come to my house around four. I'll teach you the ropes."

~ *Fourteen* ~

With her eyes full of wonderment, Margie entered Ava's bedroom. It was like entering the Emerald City. She'd never seen a room quite like it.

The soft, amber glow glimmered over the queen-size bed that was covered by a black satin comforter. Climbing almost to the ceiling, the bed posts were draped with sheer black fabric that flowed over the bed to cascade down to the floor. Huge black satin pillows were tossed near the headboard. Smaller red pillows were scattered here and there. Lying leisurely among the pillows, a large, white Persian cat stared at her with sapphire eyes. Its rhinestone collar twinkled in the soft glow.

"Pretty kitty, what's its name?" Stymied by the sensual surroundings, Margie swallowed hard.

"Stella," Ava replied.

Margie's eyes were drawn to the black lacquer vanity with a large round gilded mirror against the wall. Perfume bottles, brushes, jewelry, and make-up cases cluttered the lovely vanity. A leopard-skin stool was positioned in front of the mirror.

She breathed in deep to take in the scent of the black cherry candles burning on the night stand, window sill, and vanity. The flickering candlelight danced across the walls.

The bedroom was sensuous, and opulent, and beautiful, just like Ava. Margie couldn't take her eyes off of the radiant redhead. Her tall, slender, curvaceous body was accentuated by a clingy silver silk night-gown. Her long locks swept across her delicate pale shoulders. *How odd,* Margie thought, *for Ava to be dressed in a nightgown at four in the afternoon. Maybe not. While I lounge around in an old pair of sweats, Ava lounges in something sexy. Yep, that's the difference between perfect and well …me.*

Ava swirled a glass of chardonnay. It whipped around and around the bottom of the crystal goblet to sparkle in the candlelight.

No one drank wine at Margie's house. It was always a can of Iron City or whatever beer her father could find on sale at the Brew Threw. Even Eric drank Rolling Rock, but Margie had no trouble picturing him with a glass of wine over dinner, or in front of the fireplace while reading a novel or the newspaper.

Margie was fascinated by Ava's allure. It was little wonder why a man would want to make love to a woman like her. *That nightgown and the room would seduce any warm-blooded man. Hell, even her cat is freaking sexy. Oh yeah, Ava has much to offer and so much to teach me if I'm going to be able to compete with a woman like Jen Fleming.*

Considering where to start, Ava stood back to measure Margie from top to bottom. She opened a drawer and pulled out a container of large curlers and a curling iron, and placed them on the vanity.

Stella suddenly leapt onto the vanity. Purring, she slinked daintily amid the perfume bottles. Her long, fluffy tail lightly caressed the mirror.

Feeling antsy and in need of conversation, Margie ran her fingers over the cat's velvety fur. "Are you still seeing that cop?"

Yep, there were no secrets at the racetrack. Everyone knew everyone's business.

"Carl Lugowski?" Ava asked. "Uh, huh, I'm meeting him later for a drink. Why?"

Shrugging, Margie stroked the cat while eyeing all the beauty gadgets displayed like tiny make-up artists preparing for battle. "Just wondering."

Ava took a whiff of the chardonnay before pressing the glass to her plump, red lips to savor the last sip. With one last sweeping glance of her blank canvas, she instructed, "Take off your clothes," as casually as if she'd requested her to have a seat.

Margie's eyes popped. Her mouth dropped. "What?"

Ava tossed her a red satin robe. "Put this on. If I'm going teach you the art of seduction, you've got to dress the part, sweetie."

CȜ ȘƆ CȜ ȘƆ

Kate was waiting.

She was going to have a talk with her father, and he was going to listen. To hell with her original Eliza Doolittle scenario. *This isn't Audrey Hepburn and Rex Harrison. It's out of control. He needs to understand that he's heading toward the tutor-slash-student-slash-romantic-infatuation fiasco at warp speed.*

Lord knows, Kate had been on the receiving end of a good talking to from her father many times. "Sit in that chair, Lady Jane," he would say, in that tone that signaled, "You are sooo busted." A sermon would soon commence, which would inevitably end with confiscated car keys, extra barn duties, and the always popular, "You're grounded for two weeks." He never laid a hand on her. That was reserved for the boys.

Kate was in no position to ground her father or confiscate his car keys, but she was going to let him know what everyone at the track was thinking. *Hell, not just thinking ... saying.*

An arm reached around her to dip a finger into her homemade bar-beque sauce. The theft of the sauce was followed by a quick peck on top of her head.

"Hi, Dad." She smiled helplessly at his timing.

"Hi, baby."

The time is now. No fooling around. Put it out there while the moment is fresh. "How's the student coming along?" She brushed some of the sauce onto a chicken breast.

"She's a quick study. I'm very proud of her." Eric rummaged through the fridge.

"I see."

Somewhere between deciding on a can of soda or a Rolling Rock, he came to a dead stop. "She said, with an arched look." Opting for the beer, he closed the fridge and turned toward her. "Out with it. What's on your mind?"

If her father was nothing else, he was perceptive—very perceptive. Not really sure if she could continue, she lifted a shoulder. She kept her eyes on the chicken breasts. "Nothing."

"Good. Margie's coming here tonight."

Her reservations immediately vanished. "Dad, I like Margie, but she's way too young—"

"Whoa, are you worried that I'm becoming *involved* with her?"

Kate turned to him. "Not you—her. I've see the way she looks at you. I think she's mistaking your generosity for something more serious."

Shaking his head, he sighed. *Daughters, they worry about nothing.* "I think you're reading way too much into it."

"Wake up, Dad. God, whatta *man* you are. Haven't you noticed all the changes in Margie?" Her father's flummoxed expression told her exactly what she had been suspecting. *He's clueless. Maybe he isn't as perceptive as I thought—at least about women.* "Her appearance, Dad. Her hair is combed. Hell, it's clean. She's experimenting with make-up."

He waved his hand. "She's expanding her horizons. That's a good thing, Kate."

Her "talk" wasn't penetrating his thick skull. He wasn't getting it. "Whatever, Dad, but I think you should have a little heart-to-heart with her." She found herself looking at a totally, perplexed man.

Hokay, a change in the subject might be a good idea—before he has some sort of fatal brain freeze. She went back to schlepping the sauce over the chicken. "Anyway, I heard you're taking Jen Fleming to the benefit dance."

"How did you find that out?"

"I beat it out of Shane."

"That's loyalty for you." He rolled his eyes and made a quick exit from the kitchen—and the talk.

"It's not like I haven't seen you stop by the nurse's office," she called after him, if for no other reason than to get in the last word.

೮೩ ೮೦ ೮೩ ೮೦

Thank God for six o'clock. Before anyone else needed medical attention, or anymore paperwork called her name; Jen locked-up her office and hurried toward the parking lot.

She couldn't wait to get home, strip out of her uniform, light candles, and sink nose deep in a fragrant frothy bubble bath. She would have plenty to fantasize about in her tub tonight—Eric. He had finally asked her to the benefit dance, and she had finally tasted the lips she'd been craving for well over a year. *Oh yes, finally a foretaste of the closeness that I've been yearning for. The prospect of that intimacy is more likely now than ever before.*

Progress.

Digging through her purse for her keys, Jen noticed that the back tire of her car was flat. She groaned. Her shoulders sagged.

"Damn it, these are new tires." She bent down to inspect the damage—only to discover that both back tires had been slashed.

Standing, she noticed a note tucked in the windshield wiper. She opened it to a crudely scribbled message: *STAY AWAY FROM ERIC.*

What the hell?

"Uh, oh, what happened?" A kind soft-spoken voice startled her out of her funk. She turned to find Scott examining her flat tires with a concerned expression on his face. "Did ya run over some nails or something?"

Her nostrils flaring, Jen held the note up for Scott to see. "I don't think so."

He took the note from her. His brows pinched together. "Uh, if you've got a spare, I can at least change one of the tires for you." He handed the note back to her.

"I can call a service for the other, thank you, Scott." She pressed the button on her key to open the trunk.

Scott snatched the spare from the trunk, a tire wrench, and the jack. He wasted no time pressing the wrench into the lug nuts and flipping it in circles to loosen them.

"Who would do such a thing?" Stressing-out, Jen stared at the note in her shaking hand while her cheeks flushed.

"What happened, Jen?"

Scott's stomach twisted into a knot when he glanced over his shoulder at Ava West with her hands planted on her hips.

Jen whipped the note out for Ava to read. "They slashed my tires and left this awful note."

Ava studied the note with her left brow arched high. Her green eyes turned suspiciously toward Scott, who was now hurriedly pushing the spare tire into place. "Interesting, this looks exactly like the paper that Eric and Margie O'Conner were using at the picnic table the other day." She shoved the note in front of Scott's face. "Doesn't this look like the paper they use?"

The knot was churning into a wave of nausea. "No," he said, "that's *not* Margie's paper. I'll loosen the other tire to save time for your car service, Ms. Fleming."

Ava whipped it back to re-examine the words on the crumbled note. "It's poorly written ... like someone who's just learning to write." She gave the paper back to Jen. "Don't you think?"

Jen's narrowed eyes scrutinized the letters before glancing at Scott, who had moved to the opposite side of the car to work on the other flat tire. "I totally agree," she whispered for Ava's ears only.

"I dropped by to meet a friend at the clubhouse for a drink, but I can give you a ride home if you need one, Jen."

"Thanks, I'll be okay. The service is usually pretty fast." She dialed her cell phone.

☙ ❧ ☙ ❧

Flames flickered, crackled, and danced in the fireplace. The study was peaceful and quiet. Immersed in the newspaper, Eric relaxed to the sputter of the logs. Intrigued by a story about the daring rescue of a man wedged under a burning car, he didn't hear Kate and Margie come into the study.

"Dad, Margie's here." Kate's announcement sounded more like a warning than a statement.

"I'm sorry." Eric jerked his attention from the newspaper. "I didn't hear your car pull up."

"Dad becomes very engrossed in the paper." Kate took in Margie's unusually attractive appearance. *It's time for a reality check, for dear ol'*

Dad. My talk may not have cracked the vault, but the physical evidence might.

Margie never looked so radiant. It seemed like Eliza Doolittle herself had just walked through the damned front door.

As if a professional artist had been at work, her make-up covered flaws to bring out her most attractive feature: her dark striking eyes. Absolutely breath-taking, her hair was glossy and curly. Her new jeans were designer, to boot. Her silky pink blouse clung in all the right places—specifically, her abundant breasts.

If her father didn't soon wake up, Kate had a sinking feeling that the rain in Spain would come crashing down on the plains this evening.

"You look lovely tonight, Margie." She raised her voice. "Doesn't she, Dad?"

He snapped to attention. "Yes, yes, she does."

Margie beamed. "Thank you, Eric. Are you ready?" She placed a plate of cinnamon pastries on the coffee table. "I can't wait to be able to sit and read the paper like you, Eric." She took a seat close to him. "You've got a nice fire there."

"Yes, it's very—"

"Cozy," Margie interjected.

He glanced up at his daughter's cautionary look. "Thank you, Kate."

Sucking in her lips, her nostrils flared, Kate did an about-face and marched out of the room with a *You've-been-warned, buddy* cadence.

Eric turned to find himself nose-to-nose with Margie, who was wearing a sultry, coquettish smile. The talk he had in the kitchen with Kate suddenly hit him in the face. *She had a point. No, a very big point.*

Slowly, he drew away from her glazed-over, puppy-love expression. "Margie, I'd like to talk with you." He realized it was much too late for a rehearsed heart-to-heart, let-her-down-easy speech.

"I never got the chance to thank you for defending me against Dan Quaide the other day." Searching his face and eyes, she moved in closer.

"It was nothing."

"It was heroic, Eric. Everything you've done has been heroic. Teaching me to read and write." She smoothed her hand over his chest and felt the firmness of his biceps. Never had she even thought to touch a man this way—the way Ava had instructed. It felt so good to touch him. Ava had said it would. He was her mentor and her white knight.

The white knight was at a loss. "Education and self-esteem are—"

"The way you stood up to my father, and told him you wanted to open a new world for me—"

He grabbed her hand. His voice was hoarse. "A mind is a terrible thing to waste."

"And then that night on the porch—when he told you never to come back, but you did. That's when I knew—You were too shy or afraid to say anything—" When Eric tried to interrupt, she slipped her fingers over his mouth. "So let me say it for you. I love you, Eric West, and I know you love me."

He could have sworn he heard the front door slam, but he wasn't sure. It could have been the slamming inside of his brain. Kate was right. He didn't see it at all. Margie'd misunderstood the situation at the track with Dan. She misunderstood that he was defending her right to learn to read and write against her father's ignorance.

"Don't worry about Jen Fleming, Eric," she whispered while scooting closer to flip her leg over his lap. It was a shameless display, but it felt so good—so releasing. She had no idea that she could be so forward and frivolous. "We'll talk to her together. I'm sure she'll understand—after a while." With that, she threw her arms around him and crashed her lips onto his to unleash a passion that she had held deep inside for her entire adult life.

Eric's eyes bulged. His hands flew backward against the sofa before he clutched her waist.

"Oh, excuse us, Dad!" Mike exclaimed when he walked into the study. He grabbed Shane's arm to quickly leave the room. An epiphany exploded in their heads when they realized who their father was kissing passionately on the sofa.

The phone rang on Eric's desk.

"Wait!" Eric cried out desperately to his sons while trying to crawl out from underneath the enthralled young woman's clutches.

In wide-eyed shock at the sight of Margie twisted around their father's torso, Mike and Shane slowly turned around.

"Dad, Jen's—" Kate hurried into the room with the phone. "—on the ... phone."

Margie was glowing with passion oozing from her pores. She grinned at the West children while squeezing Eric with all her might when she said breathlessly, "I know this is a surprise, especially for you, Michael; but your father and I are in love."

Mike fell against the wall. "There's a visual that I'll never forget."

The color had drained from Eric's face. He knew what he had to do. He hated himself for not recognizing the signs. He raked a harried hand through his hair. "Guys, I need to talk with Margie—alone." He turned to Kate, whose arms were crossed. Her jaw set, she tapped her foot. "Kate, tell Jen that I'll call her in the morning."

No one was moving.

Trying to calm the nausea that was whirling in his stomach, Mike remained stationary against the wall. Kate's agitated expression held steadfast. Shane was trying to decide whether to laugh or run like hell from the room. It was a toss-up.

Finally, Eric waved his hands to shoo them from the room and closed the French doors behind them. He turned to her.

Margie was still grinning like a lovelorn schoolgirl. "I knew they'd be surprised."

He clapped his hand to the nape of his neck. "Yeah, so was I. Margie, please ... sit down."

Folding her arms around him again, she pulled him close and kissed the base of his neck. "I know it's sudden, but they'll get used to it. And don't be worried about our age difference. Lots of men marry younger women—especially when they feel needed." She laid her head against his chest and breathed in his cologne. Savoring his warmth, she listened to the thrum of his heart. "And I need you so very much, Eric."

Jesus.

His heart felt heavy for her. This time, it wasn't her father's suppression he regretted, but the heartbreak that he was about to inflict. He gave her a quick hug, and then gently he took her by the shoulders and lifted her from his chest while lowering her onto the sofa. He could barely stand the longing look in her dark eyes.

"I'm so very sorry, Margie." The words choked in his throat. "You've misinterpreted my intensions. I regret any wrong signals I may have sent you—"

She jumped up from the sofa. "Wrong signals? Oh, no, you've sent all the right ones, Eric. Defending me, teaching me—"

"Margie, I'm sorry, I don't have romantic feelings for you," he said.

She stepped back. Her lips quivered. Her dark eyes filled with anguish. "You don't?" she whispered. Tears trickled down her flushed cheeks.

"I like you, Margie, really I do—"

"*Like* me? Good God, my *cats* like me." She wiped her wet cheeks while breathing in. Rancor replaced the pain. "I should'a listened. Dad tried to warn me. 'Don't trust them Wests,' he said. 'You just ain't good enough for the likes of them.' Boy, oh boy, he hit the nail right on the head!"

"That's not true, Margie."

"Yeah, it is!" she shouted. "You high and mighty Wests, with your big Westwood Farm. How could I be so damned stupid?" She marched toward the doors.

He grabbed her by the arm. "Margie, I wanted you to learn those things so you'd have a better chance in this world. I'm too old for you. You need someone young to go through life with."

She yanked her arm from his grip. "No, Eric, I need someone to love me." She ran to the doors and grasped the knobs. She fumbled and twisted them in frustration.

"Don't throw away everything you've gained over a terrible misunderstanding."

She glared at him through her tears before flinging open the doors and bolting into the foyer where she came face-to-face with Mike, Kate, and Shane.

"This was all a big joke to you, wasn't it?" she yelped before darting out the front door.

They didn't move. They stared at the floor while listening to her old pickup starting. Spitting gravel, it ripped up the driveway. They exchanged regret-filled glances before turning toward the study. Leaning against the threshold, Eric watched the headlights twist furiously up the driveway.

Kate could see the dark remorse in his eyes. The talk hadn't enlightened him, but the physical evidence had punched him in the face. Her heart broke for him. "Dad ..."

Looking whiplashed, he shook his head, backed into the study, and closed the doors.

Part Four

An Awkward Position

Cindy McDonald

~ *Fifteen* ~

What the hell was going on?

In a tailspin, Jen looked at her condo's shattered living room window. Shards of glass covered the carpeting and the furniture. A brown brick lay in the middle of the room. A crumbled note was tied to it. The message was the same as that had found on her car only hours ago: STAY AWAY FROM ERIC. The scrawled handwriting was identical to the other warning.

Scott had insisted that the notepaper wasn't anything like the kind Margie used, but why wouldn't he deny it? *Margie was his close friend and Doug his employer.* After accepting her thanks for changing her tire, he scurried to his pickup while evading any more questions about it.

Jen wanted Eric to hold her in his strong arms and give her some kind of explanation—if he had one. Kate sounded upset when she had called Westwood to talk to him. *Maybe something similar is going on there. I hope not.*

She heard a car crunch to a stop in front of her condo. Through the jagged vestige of her front window, she could see it was the police. They were going to have questions, and she had a lead to give them.

CB ED CR ED

It was Thursday morning, but Eric wasn't sitting atop his old quarter horse, Ike, at the far end of Westwood's training track. No, this morning he was at Keystone Downs in hopes of finding Margie watching a workout. Wandering through the early morning haze, he was searching and waiting for her to appear.

No luck. I'm going to have to face it. I'm going to have to walk into the O'Conner stable, and deal with Doug. Damn it.

Bracing himself for the inevitable confrontation, he turned the corner; but, instead of Doug, he came upon a police officer leading Margie, handcuffed, to a cruiser.

At the barn door, Doug was beside himself with angst. "I'll get my lawyer." He shook his fist. "You got no proof. My Marge is a good girl. I'm gonna sue the Rosemount Police Department!"

The officer didn't care about his idle threats. He helped Margie into the backseat of the cruiser, slid into the driver's seat, and then drove away.

Doug watched with a vacant expression.

Scott shouldered past Eric with a what-the-hell look on his face.

Doug turned to Scott with tears welling in the old codger's eyes. "They're taking Marge in for questioning. They think she slashed Ms. Fleming's tires and broke her windows last night."

Scott struggled. The words slowly stammered out. "Who told them that?"

"I dunno," Doug wailed while wiping his nose on his sleeve. "They took her clipboard and her tablet." His eyes fell on Eric. Instantly, they filled with rage. "This is all your doing!" He pointed an arthritic finger in his direction.

Scott grabbed him by the shoulders. "C'mon, Doug. I'll give ya a ride to the police station. I'm sure it's a big mistake." Furtively glancing over his shoulder at Eric, he guided him toward his pickup.

Eric felt a twist of guilt in his gut. *Maybe the old crow's right. Maybe this whole debacle is my fault.* He could see in Doug's troubled eyes that he truly loved and cared about his only daughter. *He wielded subjugation, but maybe that wasn't his intention. Maybe he tried to shield his daughter from the true harm that life can impose. He's been raising a daughter without the help of a wife. It's the only way he knew how to keep the ducks in a row. It's the only way this rough-cut man knows how to help his daughter avoid the pain that he'd endured all those years ago after her mother walked out. The only way he knows how to guard her from the pain that she had experienced in these last sixteen hours.*

Yep, Doug's right. It is my fault, and I don't know what the hell to do about it.

Cʒ ઠⅅ Cʁ ઠⅅ

Strong black coffee, that's what Lieutenant Carl Lugowski needed. After running his fingers over his weary eyes, he poured the dark syrupy substance into the old chipped mug that used to be his father's. *Like father, like son.*

This mug had seen a lot of action on mornings, especially those following a long tiring night of surveillance that had amounted to squat—like this one. The only good thing about sitting in the car all night while waiting for nothing to happen was that he had a lot of time to talk with Ava. She was very good at keeping him awake. She was very good at keeping him worked up. This weekend, he was going to be very good at returning the favor.

After taking a swig, he ran the palm of his hand over his mouth, across his ear, and down the back of his neck. *Yeah, it was a long-ass night. It'll be an even longer day. No sleep. Eh, sleep is overrated, anyway.* He had a shitload of paperwork waiting at his desk, and the phones would soon be ringing off the hook. *Better get to it.*

He saw Kate West walk through the squad-room door.

He hadn't seen Kate for many months. He hadn't looked into those crystal blue eyes of hers. He hadn't had to think about the way she stirred him since he last spoke to her on the steps of the farmhouse porch at Westwood.

From the coffee machine in the break room, Lugowski watched her speak to one of the detectives. Her blonde locks drifted across her shoulders. The blue tank top she wore clung to her torso, and her jeans fit like a soft glove over her curves. *Shit. What's Mike West's little sister, Ava's ex-sister-in-law, doing here?* He was absolutely sure she had brought those mesmerizing blue eyes with her. His attraction to her was surprising, stimulating, and bothersome. The detective showed Kate to Lugowski's paper-laden desk, and had her sit in the chair next to it.

He breathed in, took another gulp of the coffee, and strolled toward her.

"Good morning, Kate," he said. "What can I do for you?" When she turned, those beautiful, blue eyes caught his breath.

"Hello, Carl, how've you been?"

Wishing for something stronger and a cigarette to boot, he looked into the contents of his mug. "I'm good. What brings you to my neck of the woods?"

Good question. She wasn't quite sure what she wanted from the lieutenant, or if he could help her at all. Last night, her father's face was a killer after Margie bolted from the house. His face was pale. He closed himself in the study for hours. She hadn't seen him so overwrought since, well, since her mother died ten years ago.

When they had heard of the vandalism done to Jen Fleming's place last evening, they were shell-shocked. She couldn't believe Margie would lash out so destructively against Jen or anyone.

It was a terrible situation at best, and she didn't know who to turn to until she remembered how gentle Lugowski had been when she needed help before. She remembered how his soothing voice had comforted her while they sipped coffee at McDonald's several months ago. Tall and slender, he was a kind man. His jaw was square and strong, and his broad shoulders carried the weight of the many victims he tended, lost, and mourned.

What is he doing with Ava? But then again, why did Mike marry her. Ava possesses a power over even the most alpha males. I wish I had that kind of power over men ... or not.

Not at all sure where she was going with it, Kate told him about Margie. She explained how her father had been tutoring her, and that Margie's interest went beyond the books without her father realizing it. She told him about Jen's tires, and her broken window, and about the notes that were found at both of the vandalisms. She also clarified that she couldn't imagine Margie being capable of such acts, and that surely there was some kind of mistake, or perhaps a cruel joke. She also informed him that the police had possession of Margie's clipboard and tablet.

Leaning back in his chair, Lugowski listened vigilantly to Kate's story while trying like hell to avoid eye contact. The sound of her voice and the movement of her hands in his peripheral vision was taking its toll. As he did months before when she needed his help, he was having the same problems focusing.

God, she drove him crazy, but in a totally different way than Ava did. Ava was sensual in a careful-when-playing-with-matches sort of way. That was a turn-on that any man could understand. Kate was sexy in a this-one's-a-keeper sort of way. That was the kind of turn-on that confuses and scares the hell out of men.

"It sounds like the damage done to the window and the tires will elevate the charges from a misdemeanor to a felony. But I don't understand what you want me to do, Kate. I'm homicide. I don't handle criminal mischief cases," he said with regret and a tug of relief.

"Can't you talk to her? You have a way of questioning people … victims, that isn't …Well, threatening." She urged a soft smile. "I remember."

He remembered, too. The first time he looked into those eyes, they were filled with terror. Again, the urge to care for her was overpowering. He didn't know what that was about. He'd handled many victims over his career. But Kate was … different.

What she was asking him to do now wouldn't be well received. "I wish I could help. But, as I said, I'm a different department. Those guys would be pissed as hell, if I stepped onto their turf."

She sat back in the chair with a sigh. "I understand." She patted his arm. "Thanks anyway, Carl."

While watching her walk out of the squad room, he reached for a pack of cigarettes from his desk drawer, tucked one in his lip, and then headed for Captain Lutz's office.

Shit, I wish I could light the damned cigarette. I can't believe what the hell I'm about to do.

03 80 03 80

Margie had never been so terrified. Her hands were shaking. Her mouth was dry. *If this is the world that Eric West was hoping to open-up for me, I'll pass. Thank ... You ... Very ... Much!*

The officer had been dead quiet in the cruiser. That was okay. She was too busy trying not to hyperventilate behind the cage in the back seat. After reaching the police station, she was fingerprinted and stuck in a small dank room. That is where she had been sitting for several hours. It seemed like an eternity.

The door knob rolled and the door jerked open.

A tall wisp of a man walked in and sat down at the table. He was followed by a frighteningly thin woman. Her dark hair was pulled back into a severe bun. She wore a white blouse and black slacks. Looking pissed as hell, she leaned against the door with her arms folded over her chest. *Thank God, she's not mad at me. She's mad at the man. Weird. Cops tend to be a tight-knit group, like it is on TV.*

The man took a moment to read the file in his hand before glancing up at her. He smiled. "Margie, I'm Lieutenant Lugowski." He hitched a chin toward the glowering woman. "And that's Detective Stewart. I spoke with Eric West a little while ago. He told me that you were at his house last evening." His voice was quiet and calm. His eyes looked like he hadn't slept in days, but there was a gentle demeanor behind his tortured appearance.

"Yes, I was," she replied.

"Can you think of anyone who would vandalize Miss Fleming's property, and make it look like you'd done it?"

"You don't think I did it?"

"No, I don't," he said.

Detective Steward couldn't suppress an eye roll.

"I didn't do anything to Miss Fleming, and I don't know who did."

He glanced up at Stewart. "Let her go."

Margie thought the woman was going to fall over. Instead she sprang into total bitch mode.

"Seriously, Lugowski?" Stewart asked through clenched teeth. "Are you forgetting that we've got the tablet with the matching paper from the notes with her prints all over them?"

"Great. You've got physical evidence of her property. But you can't put her at either scene."

"I'm sure we can find something to hold her on for a few more hours, until we—"

"Calm down, Stewart." Lugowski held up the file bearing one sheet of paper. "Look. Not so much as a traffic ticket. She's not a murder suspect. She's got an alibi. Let … her … go."

Glaring, Stewart yanked the door open and motioned for Margie to exit. She held her daggers tight on the lieutenant. "So pulled some strings with Captain Lutz, did ya?" She lowered her voice to a grouse. "Tell me, what brings you amongst us lowly run-of-the-mill, everyday, crime detectives? Bored with your bad boy murderers, Lugowski?"

He gathered the minuscule file from the table and followed Margie to the door where he tossed the detective a dry look. "Bitter? Get therapy and get over it, Stewart."

❣ ❣ ❣ ❣

After Lugowski united Margie with her father and saw them to their car, he made his way through the sea of surly faces in the station. He tugged a cigarette from his jacket pocket and pressed through the doors. He flicked his butane lighter and lifted it to the cigarette when he noticed Kate leaning a hip against the railing on the front steps of the station. A light breeze wisped through her glimmering hair. She looked the way she always looked to him. Damned tasty.

She smiled. "Thanks, Carl."

Hoping the nicotine would steady the stir, he took a long drag from the cigarette. It didn't. "Looks like you owe me, Miss West," he noted with a playful smirk.

Kate took note of the surprising grin. *Lugowski's smirking. Funny. Everyone says he's physically unable to smile, smirk, or grin. Everyone's wrong. His smirk is down-right boyish, cute … for a homicide cop, anyway.*

"Hmmm, what an awkward position to be in." She returned the grin.

"Not for me." He blew the smoke out his nostrils, tossed her a wink, and strolled toward his SUV.

~ *Sixteen* ~

Eric slammed the phone onto its base. It was the night of the benefit dance at Keystone Downs Convention Center. He'd been looking forward to taking Jen. With her, all dressed up and looking like a beauty queen, on his arm; he knew every man in the room would envy him.

Since the mix-up with Margie, he had been unable to focus. During the past week, he had tried to contact her, but she hadn't been at the track. Doug had been mysteriously absent as well.

During Eric's visits to the O'Conner stable, Scott had been indifferent to say the least. The kid refused to make eye contact with him. As if he had been submerged deep in thought, Scott continued to pitch manure into a wheelbarrow. He acted as if Eric didn't exist. For a brief moment, he would hesitate in his chore and look up like he wanted to tell him something; but then, it seemed as though he swallowed it down and changed his mind. After that, Eric couldn't pry answers, or even a passing glance, from him.

With the scene in his study running through his head, the guilt coiled in Eric's gut. He was sure Jen had noticed. She kept asking him if something was wrong. He denied it, but she knew. He knew she knew.

Dressed in a black suit, his white shirt unbuttoned, and his necktie dangling loose, he sat on the edge of his bed. Scrubbing his fingers across his freshly shaven face, he shuffled to the mirror that was mounted on the wall over his dresser. Hiking his chin, he began the task of adjusting his tie.

"Knock, knock." Kate stood in the doorway of his bedroom.

Eric smiled at his lovely daughter, who was wearing a glittering midnight blue halter gown. Her blonde hair was gathered on her head in a French twist. The diamond stud earrings in her lobes winked at him in the soft light of the room. "Don't you look beautiful?"

Kate returned his smile. "Trying to make sure you take note of things?"

He returned to the mirror and his tie. "Kinda."

Watching her father's sullen expression in the mirror, she sank onto the bed. "Can't get a hold of Margie?"

"Nope, I'll keep trying. We have to get this ironed out." The tie wasn't cooperating. He seemed to be all thumbs this evening. He flipped the ends of the tie this way and that until he finally left them to dangle around his neck in surrender.

Kate came to her father's aid. She took the ends of the tie in her hands to form a proper knot at the base of his throat. "Do you think she's capable of doing those things to Jen?"

"No, I don't," he answered, "but someone sure did. All of this over a little misunderstanding."

"A little misunderstanding to you. This was huge to her, Dad."

"I know that, Kate. I'm sure once she's settled down, and I get a chance to calmly explain, she'll understand."

Kate urged a half-smile. "I hope you're right. But, Dad, if she did those things; I know Jen'll press charges."

Dangerously dapper in a navy pinstriped suit, Shane leaned in the door. "Kate, your date is here. I'm leaving to pick up Rachel." They had no clue who Rachel was. She was probably one of the many standing in line for Shane's attention

Kate smiled to herself. *One of these days he's going to grow up, and some woman's going to bring him to his knees and put a swift end to his playboy ways—some woman that he least expected. What a grand day that would be.*

He winked at his sister. "Hey, you don't clean up half bad." With that, he skedaddled down the hall.

Smooth operator. Kate giggled. "Oh, he's such a ... Shane." She kissed her father's cheek. "I've got to go. I'll see you at the dance." She pointed a finger at him. "Don't let this ruin your evening with Jen."

His mouth turned upward while he watched her dress whirl, and glitter, and float around her when she glided out of his room. *I am truly a blessed man to have such a beautiful daughter who cares so much for me, and two strong vibrant sons to carry on the West name, and the proud racing tradition of Westwood Farm. Blessed.*

He picked up the phone and dialed again. After listening to the ring on the other end, he released a frustrated sigh before hanging up, gathered his car keys from the nightstand, and went out the door.

This is Jen's evening. She doesn't deserve to have it marred by my frustration or guilt. I need to focus on her. Hey, how hard could that be? She's a knock-out.

CB ∞ CR ∞

Jen smoothed the ginger-n-spice lipstick over her lips. She sat back in her vanity chair to admire her handiwork. She had plans for her lips tonight—especially after the dance. In the mirror, she practiced her come-hither smile that she was going to nail him with.

Tonight was her night. She owned it. She had earned it. She wasn't going to let Margie O'Conner interrupt it for one second.

Once she had Eric in the door, it would be straight to the bedroom. No detours. She didn't want him in the living room with the boarded-up window. It would only make him feel bad, and that wasn't what she wanted him to feel tonight. *Oh, no, tonight it's going to be about the two of us between my cool blue sheets. Mmm, it will be so good feeling the heat, and the sensual friction between our naked bodies. Tonight is going to be about unbridling the intimacy I've been fantasizing about for so long.*

The Miracle Bra she was wearing pushed a pleasing cleavage from her satin emerald gown's sweetheart neckline. She dabbed a touch of perfume between her breasts and smiled about the bra's perky performance. *Oh, yes, tonight will be the night.*

CB ∞ CR ∞

The enormous ballroom was decked-out with pink, blue, purple, and white helium balloons that floated, bumped, and danced along the high ceiling. Draped in white linen, each table sported huge arrangements of pink calla lilies in glass vases in its center. A Michael Buble song played in the background while guests chatted, laughed, and enjoyed hors d'oeuvres served by waiters.

Mike was with an attractive brunette that Kate had insisted he would "get along with very well," whatever that meant. He had hoped to be at the dance with Coco. After she took up with Tom Mason, Mike decided to stay home and do some paperwork. Kate wasn't having it. Ignoring his objections and always knowing what was best for the West men, she had made a phone call.

Thanks, sis.

He thought the girl's name would be Eliza, but it turned out to be Tanya. He was relieved. *What kind of a name was Eliza Doolittle, anyway?*

A mere five-foot-two, Tanya was tiny, and couldn't have weighed more than one-hundred-and-ten pounds while soaking wet. She was small enough to be a jockey. *Yikes.*

She's ... cute. I don't do cute. What the hell was Kate thinking? I like tall leggy women. I like a woman with curves. Breasts are always nice. This girl has what looks to be dried-up prunes. I like a woman I can wrap my arms around and not feel like she'll break in half.

Her one-shouldered red dress was adorable. She wore her brunette hair swept back into a ponytail to expose the sparkling rhinestone hoops dangling from her earlobes.

Tanya was chatty. She talked and talked and talked. She had a fondness for twenty questions and she fired them off like a machine gun. "Do you like being a horse trainer?" "How long have you been a horse trainer?" "Do you make a lot money at that?" "Are the Thoroughbreds the one's with the tiny saddle?" And his personal favorite question of the evening: "So, how long were you married to your wife? Are you divorced or just separated?"

God, when will this dance be over? She's short, she's flat, and she talks way too much. I may have a hard time forgiving Kate for this one. I'll have no problem forgetting this chick ever existed.

155

Mike thought his head was going to explode by the time his father and Jen arrived at the table. Eric pulled a chair out for Jen. "What can I get you to drink?"

"I'll have a zinfandel. Thank you."

Mike almost knocked over his chair when he jumped up. "I'll come with you."

Eric waved his hand. "No, you stay and get acquainted with your date." He smiled at her. "Can I get you something?"

"I'm Tanya. I'll have a rum and Coke. Thank you. Are you Mike's dad?"

"Yes, I'm Eric—"

"Are you a horse trainer, too?"

Eric noticed his son's peeved expression. "A zinfandel, and a rum and Coke, it is."

While he maneuvered around the table, he heard Tanya ask Jen, "Are you Mike's mom?"

Poor Mike, what the hell was Kate thinking? He scanned the room for Shane or Kate while making his way to the bar. "A white zinfandel, rum and Coke, a Rolling Rock ..."

He glanced back at the table. Mike was leaning on his elbow with his head cupped in his hand. Tanya's lips were still moving. He needed a rescue. "And give me a double shot of your best whiskey," he instructed the bartender.

Leaning in close, Dan Quaide squeezed his shoulder. "Jen's looking damned hot tonight, ole boy. Much better choice than that O'Conner girl."

Eric's jaw locked.

Dan didn't know when to quit. "Hey, maybe I'll ask Jen for a dance later."

With a warning in his eyes, Eric turned to him. "Maybe I'll break your jaw later."

The left side of Dan's mouth turned upward when he looked past Eric's shoulder. His eyes brightened. "Don't look now, buddy, but you've got double trouble." With a sleazy grin toward the ballroom doors, he hiked his chin.

Eric turned to see Margie walk in on Scott Carter's arm.

Wearing a plain black sheath dress, she looked good. Her hair fell around her shoulders in a cascade of curls.

Eric was most impressed with Scott. He didn't look bad in a nice grey suit.

The bartender handed Eric his drink order on a small tray.

After tossing several bills on the bar, he shouldered past Dan toward Margie. He walked up behind her. "Margie, how are you?"

Producing a pleasantly forced smile, she turned to him. "I'm good, Eric, how about you?"

"I'm fine. I've been trying to bump into you all week."

"I heard."

"I wanted to iron some things out with you," he said.

Margie was eyeing-up the tray of drinks in Eric's hand. Her lips curled. "Is that wine for Jen?"

He shot her a perplexed expression. "Yes, yes, it is."

She took the wine glass from the tray and guzzled it down. "Mike would'a hated calling me mom, anyways." Leaving Eric without his zinfandel order, she led Scott into the ballroom.

Φ &#x07F; Φ &#x07F;

The evening belonged to Jen. She owned it. Well, almost. Eric complimented her dress and her hair. Except when he glanced in Margie's direction, she had his undivided attention. She could tell he was bothered by the whole vandalism situation. *No worries. Once I have him alone at my place, the Margie O'Conner distractions will cease to exist. Oh yes, I have every intention to drive him to distraction, all right. Lights low, candles lit, and clothes scattered on the floor.*

Then, there was the other diversion: The fact that Shane never showed-up. Kate called him several times—no answer.

Kate's date was a real hottie. Holden Reese was a big guy. With broad shoulders, he was tall at six-foot-one, if not taller. He carried a rugged cowboy air about him. With dark-colored hair, he wore a dark chocolate suit with light brown stitching that formed curly yokes at the shoulders. Hot damn, it was definitely working for him.

Jen wasn't surprised. *Who else would Kate attract but Mister Tall-Dark-and-Incredibly-Gorgeous?*

On the other hand, Mike doesn't seem to be enjoying his date at all. I don't know why. Tanya's a little cutie. She's very personable, talkative, and perky. Okay, maybe a little too perky.

Mike seemed very put-off. Jen surmised that it might be because his ex-wife, Ava, looked so dazzling while dancing close with the tall, slender gentleman who she had brought to the dance. She noticed that Ava's date stealthily glanced in Kate's direction every once in a while. *Who can blame him? She's truly striking.*

Then, there was the blonde bombshell, Coco Beardmore, who Mike kept eyeing-up as well as he was his ex-wife. *Seems Eric's elder son has an attraction to tall beautiful women. He seems annoyed to see her with Tom Mason, a much older, but well-maintained, man.*

Nope, poor Tanya really isn't cutting the mustard.

In the far corner of the ballroom, Coco was attracting a crowd. Kate elbowed Mike and the entire table went to see what the commotion was about. They eddied into the circle that had formed around her. Next to a table decked-out with fine china and crystal, she sparkled in her black strapless gown. Beaming at his date, Tom Mason seemed intrigued by what the bombshell had in store for everyone.

"Are you ready, everybody?"

She waited for the crowd to respond with a hearty, "Yes!"

Coco laughed and clapped her hands. "Okay, this is my party trick."

Expecting the worst, Mike bit his lip. Eric and Kate braced, too.

Coco nodded to the DJ, who played a drum roll over the sound system. She took a firm hold of the linen tablecloth beneath the china and the crystal, and yanked quick and hard.

The crowd cheered. Undisturbed, every piece of china and crystal remained in their original positions. Tom grabbed his talented date and kissed her.

Over the roar of the zealous crowd, Jen heard Mike lean into Kate. "Seriously? The woman can't cook dinner without causing a three-alarm fire, but she can pull off that freaking party trick?"

"Look around, Mike, she has caused a fire," Kate pointed out.

Mike measured the faces in the crowd. *Hell, even Lugowski's smiling and clapping. Oddly, he's staring at Kate. Now what the hell is that about?*

The lights dimmed, and the music went low and slow.

Eric pulled Jen close. She ran her hands up and down his arms while breathing in his cologne and the warmth of his body against hers. The evening had been as she hoped, but it was time to get the late night festivities ignited.

"Eric, I've had a wonderful time," she whispered, "but my feet are killing me." *Hope that's not too transparent.* "How about if we go to my place, so I can get out of these heels."

"Will I be allowed to loosen my tie?"

"Oh, yes, by all means."

"Then you're on." He gestured to Kate that he was leaving.

Holding back the urge to break into a dead run, Jen led him from the dance floor. On their way out of the ballroom, she scooped up her purse when they passed the table. They went out to the lobby.

Jen hesitated at the ladies room. "I'll be right back." She kissed his cheek before disappearing through the door.

Eric wasn't waiting until they arrived at Jen's condo. *I'm loosening this damned tie this very instant. Enough with the choking already.*

Margie rounded the corner and bumped into him.

"Margie ..."

She smiled. "I signed my name yesterday for the UPS man."

"I'm glad to hear that."

"Thanks."

"Margie—" Not wanting to participate in whatever conversation he wanted to start, she waved her hand and made a quick escape into the ladies room.

CB EO CA EO

Jen smacked her lips together in the mirror, they were plump and moist and ready for action. Assuring that her breasts were perfectly primed, she tugged at her dress. *Eric West is going to get the ride of his life tonight.*

Standing behind her, Margie appeared in the reflection of mirror. Her face was stiff and her eyes were razor sharp.

Jen's eyes widened. She dropped her lipstick into her evening bag and turned to make a swift exit.

Margie blocked her path. "I wanna talk to you."

Jen squared her shoulders. "About what? My slashed tires or my broken window?"

"What?"

Jen hitched her chin while rolling her eyes. "Don't act like you don't know what I'm talking about." She tried to sidestep around her, but Margie stepped in front of her again.

"I wanna talk about Eric—"

"You can talk to my attorney." Jen shoved her aside and reached for the door.

Margie grabbed her arm. "Wait a minute."

Jen wasn't interest in waiting for anything. *I'm not buying Margie's lame act of the poor, innocent, brow-beaten daughter of Doug O'Conner. She may have fooled Eric but not me. I'm not going to let her get away with it any longer.* She yanked her arm from Margie's grip and slapped her hard across the face.

Margie's head snapped to the side. Her eyes bulged and her mouth dropped open. *Whatta bitch!* She cuffed her in the jaw.

CB ED CR ED

Eric's tie drooped through his collar. He had even unbuttoned the top three buttons of his shirt. *Relief.* He leaned against the wall, checked the time on his watch, and sighed. That was when he heard a thump against the ladies room door. He jolted away from the wall and listened intensely to the harsh voices wafting from behind the door. He could hear a skirmish. He crept toward the door with his eyebrows furrowed. The aggressive movements and the agitated voices were louder and more severe.

Desperately, he looked around the lobby. It was empty and quiet. The only sounds were the low murmur of the crowd and the romantic music from the ballroom … and the callous voices rising rigorously from the bathroom.

Sweat beaded on his forehead as panic scraped up his spine. He stepped toward the ladies room door, reached for the handle, and then retreated.

He looked around the lobby again. It was still empty. He swallowed hard. He'd never been in a ladies room. That was a place where women did ... women things ... a no-man's land. While most men wondered what the hell are they doing in there, what the hell's taking so long, and why do they always visit that room in pairs; it was still a place men regard as "off limits."

The murmur of loud voices grew harsh, which graduated to yelling, and then another hard thump followed by several *bang, bedunk, clang, clangs*. The yelling changed to screaming, screeching, and what sounded like skidding.

Jesus.

It was time to toss his inhibitions aside. He grabbed the handle and dashed into the mysterious forbidden no-man's land. He slid to a stop at the end of the short row of stalls. He couldn't believe his eyes.

An entanglement of bodies, Jen and Margie were rolling over the floor, pulling hair, kicking, and shrieking. Jen's lovely gown was bunched around her waist. The shoulder of Margie's dress was ripped.

Jen kicked her leg furiously against a stall door, which bounced open and then slammed closed. *Bang! Bedunk! Clang! Clang!*

"What the hell is going on?" Eric shouted.

They weren't listening. Jen had her hand cupped under Margie's jaw, which forced her head against the floor. Meanwhile, Margie was yanking Jen's head backwards by her hair.

The stall doors reverberated. *Bang! Bedunk! Clang! Clang!*

This was a major cat fight. Some men may have been totally turned on by the female fury. Eric? No so much. His face was flushed and the beads of sweat were now streams running down his temples. He had to do something. Straddling the women, he forced them apart and lifted them to their feet. It was poor judgment on his part, or perhaps he didn't realize the scope of the situation. He braced himself between the two snarling women.

The silence was brief.

Anger rushing through her veins, Jen lurched forward at Margie. Trying to block the blow, Eric caught Jen's swift right hook to the jaw. Margie obviously considered this a cheap shot. Arms pumping, she desperately tried to get a good hold of Jen's hair but came up with a chunk of Eric's instead.

"Stop!" Eric shrieked.

Just then, several women wondered into the room. They gasped at the sight of the two women with their hair askew, dresses ripped, and blood dripping from Jen's nose. Eric looked like a madman with his mussed hair, a steady trickle of blood dribbling from his lip, and his arms firmly wrapped around Jen and Margie's waists.

The women's eyes popped and their faces filled with fright. Calling him disparaging names, they threw their purses at Eric. Some threw the contents of their bags. He ducked and dodged. Some of the purses hit him in the head and shoulders. Others missed him to hit the stall doors. *Bang! Bedunk! Clang! Clang!*

Enough was enough. Eric had had his fill of the mysterious room. Tucking Jen and Margie under each arm, he dashed around the panicked women into the now crowded lobby. He set the infuriated women down only to realize that he was surrounded by a mass of shocked, wide eyed on-lookers.

A familiar voice rang out. "Whoa, Eric. What have you been up to?" Dan could barely get the words out for his laughter.

Followed by Kate, Holden, and Tanya, who was suddenly speechless; Mike pushed through the crowd.

Mouth gaping open, Scott pushed to the front to take in the sight of the trodden women.

Jen ripped away from Eric's grip. "I'm going home."

"I'll take you," he insisted.

Her face was flushed beyond embarrassment. "No, I can find my own way home, thank you very much." She brushed back a lock of hair from her eyes. With one shoe missing, she limped through the crowd.

When Margie turned to leave in the other direction, Scott grabbed her arm. "I'm sorry." He swallowed hard. His voice was thick with guilt. "This is my fault." He turned to Eric. "I slashed Ms. Fleming's tires. I threw the brick through her window."

Once again, Margie's face filled with hurt. Tears came to her dark eyes. "Why, Scott? Why would you do such an awful thing and let them blame me?"

His mouth moved but no words came out. He didn't know what he expected.

I never expected it to go this far. I just wanted to put a huge wedge between Margie and the Wests. I never thought anyone would get arrested or charged. Then again, I've never done anything like vandalism before. Maybe I didn't think it through enough. I just wanted Margie back at the dances with me. Truth be told, I just wanted Margie to be with me, period. But how can I tell her that now? I damned well can't.

Shrugging his shoulders, he dropped his gaze to the floor.

Astounded that he had no explanation, no reason, and no words, Margie took a step back. The lobby was caving in on her. She felt the weight of betrayal waging down upon her. Eric didn't love her. Mike wouldn't touch her with a ten-foot pole; and now Scott was nothing more than a coward, a liar, and a dirty vandal.

Eric's rumpled appearance broke Kate's heart, but Margie's broken soul was more than she could bear. Her father was strong. He could get himself home. She wasn't so sure about Margie.

She took Holden's arm and stepped forward. "C'mon, Margie, we'll drive you home," she whispered while taking her by the shoulders.

"Wait." Colette stepped from the crowd. "I'll take her home, Kate. Margie and I are old friends."

Colette's eyes were filled with a watery compassion that took Kate aback. She stepped aside so that Colette could lead Margie away from the humiliating situation. Margie willingly went with her shoulders sagging and the top of her dress torn to hang below her bra. Pulling his car keys from his jacket, Tom Mason followed.

As they made their exit, Kate glanced over her shoulder. Lugowski had approached Scott to inform him that he was under arrest.

03 80 03 80

It was almost midnight when Tom drove up to a stop in front of the O'Conner's farm. His eyes popped at the unkempt conditions. When Colette grasped the door latch to get out, he touched her arm firmly and whispered, "Are you sure you want to go in there? Is it safe for me to leave my car here?"

Colette's half smile was definite. She patted his hand. "It will be fine, Tom." She wasn't as confident as she was putting on. While they made their way up the sidewalk, Colette could see Doug, peering out the front window from behind the threadbare curtains.

As if he expected a werewolf or a chainsaw murderer to jump out from the twisted, overgrown trees in the chicken-scratched yard, Tom searched the entire area.

Margie was a mess. Her dress was torn, her hair was askew, and her mascara had dried in long black streaks where her tears had fallen down her swollen cheeks.

Even that rat-bastard father of hers could see that she needed a heavy dose of TLC from a woman who understood. When he opened the door to see Colette and Tom standing there with Margie, Doug stepped aside to let Colette enter the house and take Margie to her bedroom.

Colette was relieved that he didn't say a word.

In the bedroom, Colette reached for the light switch inside the door.

"Leave it," Margie muttered in a morbid tone while peeling the ruined dress from her shoulders and dropping it to the floor. She yanked back the blanket from her bed and plunked down. She wrapped her arms around her legs and dropped her face into her knees.

Colette glanced around the room.

The moonlight filtered through a pair of white sheers with purple butterflies. The wall beside the bed was cracked diagonally from the top corner of the ceiling to the far corner of the floor. Without more than three or four-feet of space between them, an old dresser rested against the wall across from her bed. Almost barren, the room was null and void of décor or even personal belongings. No indeed, Margie was not accustomed to any frills.

She ran her fingers lightly through Margie's hair. "It's going to be okay," she soothed. "I know how you feel."

Margie's head jerked up. "How's that possible? How could someone like you even begin to know how I feel?" Her tears had begun to flow again. Her voice was ripped with frustration. "Look at you. You're freaking gorgeous. Men fall all over you. So don't tell me that you know how I feel, Coco."

Colette let out a thin snort. "You're right. Men do react to me, but for all the wrong reasons. Beauty isn't always a gift, and neither is wealth. Men love my looks, but they fall *in love* with my money."

"Even Mike West?"

"Mmmm, he liked my looks … hated my horses." She giggled. To her surprise and delight, Margie managed a giggle through her tears.

Colette picked up her purse from the floor and pulled out a wet-nap. She washed the mascara from under Margie's eyes and cheeks. "You're eyes are naturally beautiful, Margie. You don't need all that gunk on them. You're lucky."

Not feeling very lucky, Margie lay back onto the pillow. Colette pulled the blanket over her. She was most grateful to Coco for bringing her home; but she felt the need to be alone, to sort things out and, yeah, to wallow in self-pity.

"You don't have to stay. I'll be okay. Thanks for everything."

"Hey, you took care of me not long ago, remember? That's what friends are for."

Tugging the blanket over her shoulder, Margie stared into the darkness of her room. The exhaustion of heartbreak consumed her to lull her to sleep.

&#x03; € &#x03; €

It had been over an hour since Colette disappeared into the ramshackle house. Tom waited patiently. God bless him, he sat among the sleeping cats on the steps of the O'Conner's porch with his allergies in full smack-down. His eyes watered. Sniffing and sneezing, wheezing and snorting while praying that his throat didn't close, he sucked desperately on his inhaler. Spitting tobacco juice over the railing while rocking in his chair, Doug's severe scowl bore into his spine.

There were two places in the world that Tom didn't want to die: a Walmart parking lot and this God-forsaken place.

Despite the awkward unpleasant company, and the tightening in his throat, Tom waited for Colette to emerge from the house. Finally, the moment arrived. The screen door screeched open and she stepped onto the porch.

Doug rocked forward in his chair. "Marge okay?"

Colette tossed him a steely glance. "No … but she will be."

She was shocked at Tom's decayed condition. Using his silk tie as a handkerchief, he tossed her the keys to his Mercedes. "You drive," he managed in a breathless, sandpaper voice.

"Poor baby." She took him by the shoulders and guided him toward the car with several cats following along.

~ *Seventeen* ~

Kate wasn't sure if she should be worried or annoyed. *Where the hell is Shane?* She thought as she drove along the road toward Keystone Downs.

The testosterone terror hadn't shown up at the dance last night, nor was he in the kitchen pouring coffee into his travel mug for breakfast before she left for the track.

Maybe this Rachel-girl had him tied to a bed post somewhere. She chuckled. *It would serve him right. Hmmm, how would that telephone conversation go? "Hey Mike, I'm a little tied-up right now, could you cover my chores, like all day?"* The thought made her laugh out loud. Try as she might, she couldn't quite come up with what Mike's exact reaction would be.

She sighed. Her date with Holden Reese had gone perfectly. They danced. They talked. They flirted. He looked so damned hot in his western-style suit. He smelled all musky and manly and sexy as hell. *No problem picturing myself in the throws of passion with him. No sirree. No sweat ... or yes, sweat, lots and lots of sweat. Mmmm, Mmmm, Mmmm.*

Yep, everything was going great until all hell broke loose in the lobby with her father smack-dab in the middle of it. She hoped that Holden wasn't terrified that all dates with Kate West were like that.

Promising that he'd call, he kissed her tenderly, not passionately, at the front door in his haste to leave. *Red flag.*

Needing a fresh cup of coffee, she rolled her new, new Mustang into a parking spot in front of the Stop-N-Shop convenience store, next to Shane's Jeep Wrangler.

Well, well, the golden boy cometh. She chuckled when she pressed through the door and spotted him filling his travel mug in the back corner of the store. He didn't look any worse for the wear. He was wearing a fresh pair of Levi's and a clean T-shirt. Lordy, he never fails to amaze her. He must keep a go-bag in his Jeep among other things that she didn't want to know about. *Smooth operator, indeed.* He was pouring the columbian coffee so she took a spot at the next dispenser to fill her cup with hazelnut coffee.

"Rachel wasn't up to coming to the dance?" she asked with a drummed-up tone of concern.

A devilish playboy grin formed on his lips. "She liked my suit."

"Really?" she asked wryly.

"What can I say? I'm freaking irresistible."

"And humble. Don't forget humble."

He twisted his mug closed. "On my way to the track." He glanced at his watch. "Doc Spears is gonna be pissed if you're late." He tossed the cashier two bills and hurried out the door.

He was right, the old track veterinarian that she worked for as a vet assistant was a real stickler for starting his rounds by seven o'clock.

She poured creamer into her coffee, but the aroma of hazelnut wasn't nearly as strong as the musky men's cologne wafting through the air. *It smells just like … Holden.* Expecting her tall, hot cowboy, she turned.

Wrong.

Carl Lugowski wore that same boyish grin he had displayed outside the police station the week before. Surprisingly, she still found it cute, homicidal cute anyway.

"I saw your new Mustang parked outside. Nice," he said.

"I'm not double parked or anything, am I? I mean, you're not going to give me a ticket, are you?" Accompanied with plenty of snarky attitude, she planted her hands on her little sexy hips.

Lugowski liked it. *Not only is she a keeper, this girl has sass.* "Let's review. I'm homicide and you still owe me." He tossed his own brand of snarky in her direction, just for the shit of it.

She hitched her chin. "Still awkward."

"Still don't care."

Ↄ ⁋ Ↄ ⁋

How did everything get so screwed up? Two short months ago, Margie's whole life revolved around her barn chores. *It was simple. Dad and me and the horses and Old Country Gold playing on the radio. Simple. Now? Not so much. Now, I have feelings I don't know what do with. Now, I have so much heartache that I'll never be the same. I'll never trust another man, other than Dad, ever again.*

Raking her fingers through her hair, Margie sank onto a bale of straw and buried her face in her hands. Hot tears rolled down her cheeks. Funny, she had cried so much last night into her pillow that she thought surely there could be no more tears left. Sniffling, she wiped her face on her old faded oversized flannel shirt.

"Hey, Margie." Mike's voice startled her, which instantly pissed her off. Not her usual reaction, to say the least. Things were different now—much different.

"What do you want?" There was no excitement in her voice. There was no glazed-over, puppy love look in her eyes. Rancor ... that's what Mike was facing now.

"I just want to talk." He sat down onto the bale next to her.

Glaring, she scooted to the other end of the bale and folded her arms over her chest. "Careful, you ain't got your ten-foot pole with you."

Okay, I deserve that. Leaning forward, Mike rested his elbows on his knees and shoved a piece of straw between his teeth. "My dad's feeling pretty bad about what happened."

"He should."

He looked her in the eye. "Really? Why? The man took time to teach you something that you will use for the rest of your life. Okay, he didn't have feelings for you. So what? You owe him more than a cold shoulder, Margie. Don't you think?"

"He thought I did those terrible things to Jen Fleming."

"No, he didn't. He defended you, believed in you. The least you could do is give him what he needs now ... peace of mind. Or maybe, if you can find it in yourself, a simple thank you."

She fell forward and hid her face in her hands. "You're right, Mike," she wept. "He was wonderful. I'm just so messed-up right now."

His heart felt heavy for her. He bit his lip. Fingers spread wide; he gently caressed her back with the palm of his hand. He could feel the tremors of her weeping.

Tears streaming from her dark eyes, she sat up. "I'll talk to him, Mike. I promise." She wiped her nose again on her shirt. "What do I do with Scott?"

Wow, tough question. He remembered the look in Scott's eyes the day he had bumped into him at O'Conner's stable. He didn't recognize it then, but he saw the same look on Scott's face at the dance when Margie asked him why he had framed and humiliated her. It was becoming all too clear to Mike what Scott Carter was feeling.

"Scott's the one, Margie. He's the one who has feelings for you. Take it from me, sometimes forgiveness is a tough thing to muster up. And forgetting? Well, you have to find the forgiveness first. Hopefully, the forgetting will come … with time."

ɔʒ ʃɔ ɔʃ ʃɔ

She blew it. No, he blew it. No, Margie O'Conner blew it right out of the damned water. The little bitch may as well have had a grenade.

Jen's magic evening was blown to smithereens. She and Eric had never made it to her place, and never made it to the bedroom where her plans to strip him out of that suit and rock his world never happened.

Margie's plans? Well played, well executed, and well … she won. Touchdown.

Jen let out a pathetic chuckle.

If Clay were here, he'd dub the entire fiasco as FUBAR: Fucked Up Beyond All Recognition. It was a military term.

Clayton Marshall, her ex-husband, was military to the bone, Marines. He referred to everything in military terms. Assigned to an ops unit, he was often far away from home, usually in some third-world country, for long periods of time. When he did come home; he was distant and absent. Their sex life was fast, wicked, and unfeeling. He treated their son, Brandon, as if he were one of his soldiers. It was as if the missions that he served on had stolen his spirit to render him incapable of tender intimacy, even love.

It had been a dozen years since the divorce. Neither Brandon nor she had heard one word from Clay. Oftentimes, on sleepless nights, she wondered if his body was rotting in a jungle somewhere. Shuddering, she would force herself to deem, "He's not my problem, not my concern, and he's not my husband anymore."

Leaning her elbows on the vanity, Jen dropped her face into her hands and laced her fingers through her hair. She had thought Eric would be the new beginning she so desperately needed and wanted. *What the hell happened? I was alone in the ladies room, putting on my lipstick and a nanosecond later, I was rolling over the bathroom floor with Margie on top of me. The rest is a blur. Thank God.*

After hiding in a ladies room on the far side of the Convention Center while speculating where her other shoe might be, she called a taxi and got home at two in the morning.

Her cell phone vibrated in a tiny circle on the vanity top. *INCOMING CALL: ERIC WEST.*

Even through the night, he had been ringing her phone every couple hours.

She couldn't talk to him. *Not now. I'm too embarrassed. I don't know how I'm ever going to face him, again.*

The phone went to voice mail. He had left three, maybe four messages, but she hadn't listened to any of them.

Yeah, I know what he probably wants to say, "I'm sorry, Jen, I can't see you anymore. Why? Because you're a total asshole." Trying to shake that image out of her mind, she shivered.

No, not Eric's style, he's too much of gentleman. He'll probably say, "I'm sorry, it's just not working out. I'm really not ready for a committed relationship." Then, he'll kiss me on my forehead and walk out of my life forever. If that little hillbilly whore has her way; he'll walk right into hers. That was the image she really needed to shake off.

Well, so much for progress, and so much for the prospect of a new beginning.

She slumped back into her chair to stare at the reflection of her weary face in the mirror. She focused on the tiny laugh-lines around her eyes and mouth. Character, that's what her mother used to say that they represented. The character of a woman's life.

Mom was right. Okay, enough with the feeling sorry for yourself, Jennifer Fleming. You're still an attractive charismatic woman. Don't let that poser take your man. That's right. Your man.

Her cell phone bumped and jiggled on the vanity. If it was Eric, she was going to answer it and she wasn't going to let him break it off. *Oh, no, I'm going to pull out my claws and fight like a tiger.* When she grabbed the phone, it wasn't Eric.

INCOMING CALL: MARGIE O'CONNER.

Good. Let's get down to brass tacks, bitch.

CB   ED   CR   ED

What the hell was I thinking? I ruined any chance I ever had with Margie.

Scott mulled over the events of the past day. They had fun at the dance. They were talking and laughing. They even slow danced once or twice. He thought they were making progress. It was slow, but it was steady progress. She was forgetting all about Mike West and Eric? Well, that could be written-off as a huge misunderstanding.

Mistakes are supposed to be part of the dues one pays for a full life. Whoever said that must have really thought through every mistake they ever made.

Scott shoveled another heap of horseshit into a wheelbarrow in Dan Quaide's stable. Yep, he was now working for Dan. He could never go back to the O'Conner stable. Doug would most likely be waiting for him with a shotgun. *Hell, he probably hates me worse than Mike West—no contest. Eh, I can't blame him. I deserve it. Margie deserves better and I've failed miserably.*

He should've admitted to the vandalism to Eric West when he stopped by the stable looking for Margie. *At least, it would have been done in private instead of in front of all those people at the dance. It would have been less humiliating and hurtful for Margie. Poor Marge, she was the one that ended up the big loser in the whole quandary.*

The guilt was suffocating.

"Thought they'd have you locked up." Margie's voice caught him off-guard.

Surprised not only to see her but that she would even speak to him without launching some heavy projectile in his direction, Scott looked up.

He leaned the pitchfork against the wall and stuffed his hands into his pockets. His face felt flushed and hot. "I've got a hearing in two weeks," he said into his chest with a lift of his shoulder. He wasn't able, nor did he want, to look at her.

Margie noticed a book sitting on top of a bucket with a picture of George Washington on the cover. Scott had mentioned that he liked historical books. He wasn't a stupid man. It was generational poverty that kept him mucking-out stalls and living in the trailer park across the street from the racetrack.

They weren't worldly people. They weren't well-traveled or well-spoken. They belonged to the racetrack. For Scott, it was a prison. For Margie, it was the only place she knew. For both, it was home. Yep, they were cut from the same cloth.

"So what do you think is gonna happen?" She tried to hide it, but concern bled into her voice.

He looked up, and was shocked to find empathy in those dark exotic eyes that belonged to the woman he had fallen in love with, had hurt, and had humiliated. *I don't deserve what I see. Concern? Could it be? Is that forgiveness I'm looking at?*

"I'll probably have to pay Ms. Fleming restitution. Maybe do some public service for a while. We'll see." He still wondered what was going on behind those incredible eyes.

"Mmmm, so what are you doing here?"

"Mucking stalls for Dan."

"We got plenty of stalls that need mucking."

Now he was totally baffled. *How can she invite me back after everything I've done to her?* He dragged his gaze to meet hers. Her eyes were smiling at him. *Smiling. Damn, she's a strong woman. Is she strong enough to forgive?* He couldn't imagine, but something made him step past the wheelbarrow. Something gave him the courage to step toward her, until he was close—very close.

She sucked in her lips and gave way to a cock-eyed grin. "Unless you'd rather muck stalls for Quaide." She looked away. "I'd like it if you came back to our stable." She lifted her gaze to meet him square in the eye.

He couldn't breathe. His heart flipped inside his chest. He grabbed her and, God help him, he kissed her the way he had wanted to kiss her for weeks.

She didn't pull away. Closing her eyes, she kissed him back, because she knew the kiss was sincere. It was a kiss she'd been waiting for thirty-three long years.

"Are you sure, Margie?" he whispered with his forehead pressed against hers. His lips still touched hers.

How strangely wonderful. A conversation. Lip to lip. "I am." Wanting another taste of his sincerity, she pressed her mouth against his.

Slowly, he drew away. "You've forgiven me?"

"No, but I'm working on it."

CB EO CR EO

Ava was making herself comfortable. She propped her feet up on Jen's desk, crossed her left leg over her right, leaned back in the chair, and dragged her fingers through her silken hair.

Trying to stay busy, Jen had come to the office to get some work done while keeping a calm demeanor until her visitor arrived. She looked lean and mean in her navy slacks, and pristine white blouse with a patch over the left breast pocket that read: Keystone Downs Medical Team.

Jen didn't expect a stopover from Ava. But there she was, and she was hunkering down for a lengthy stay.

"Take it from me, Jen. Those West boys are more trouble than they're worth." Bullets, Ava loved to make bullets. "I can't believe Eric would play around with someone so much younger, and yet so ... well, you know, unattractive."

Conceding that trying to get anything done would be futile, Jen tossed her pen onto the pile of paperwork. "Men love younger women, and that seems to be the norm. But I can't believe he'd go for someone so aggressively vindictive."

"What do you mean?"

"My car, my window, remember?"

Cupping her hand to her mouth, Ava gasped. "You don't know. Margie didn't do those things. Scott Carter did. He admitted to it at the dance." Her eyes widened. "Oh, it was after you'd left."

Oops! Now she'd have to make a different kind of bullet. Not a problem. Landing on her feet, she regrouped. "She was still trying to get her hooks into Eric. You know, I'm not so sure she wasn't successful. You've got to give her credit—playing the part of the closet illiterate ... smart, very smart."

Jen had stopped listening at "*Margie didn't do those things. Scott Carter did ...*" She couldn't believe it. He was so nice to her after she found her tires slashed. *Oh, God, I've been duped.* Her stomach was feeling weak.

When Margie walked through her office door, Ava whipped her feet off of the desk. Jen stiffened in her chair.

"Well, I'd better be going. Doc Spears will be looking for me. He wanted extra help today." Ava was wide eyed.

"Oh, you don't have to go, Ava," Jen prodded with a sly grin.

Ava scurried passed Margie. "No, no, like I said, Doc's waiting." With that, she rushed out the door.

She took several steps. It was killing her. *What's Margie doing here? A smile crept across her lips. Another cat fight?* She just had to know. She waited outside to hear the fireworks that she was confident would soon begin.

Jen leaned back in her chair with her eyes trained on Margie. "Okay, you're here."

"How would Eric put it? 'Let's iron this out.'" Margie crept to the door, grabbed the knob, and shoved it open sharply.

The door smacked Ava in the face and tossed her backward to the floor. *K-thump!* Blood streamed from her nostril, down her chin, and onto her T-shirt. She was dazed. The coppery taste of blood filled her mouth. Grabbing her nose, she scrambled to her feet and scurried for a rest room.

Sneering, Margie closed the door. Smirking, Jen stood up.

Margie reached into her back pocket and produced a glittery, silver, sling-back shoe. She tossed it onto the desk. "Found your shoe. Thought ya might want it back."

Jen snickered. "Thanks. So ... let's iron this out ..."

"Woman to woman." Margie happily agreed.

~ *Eighteen* ~

Concentration was eluding Eric. He'd been trying to read the newspaper for the past hour and a half, but the events at last evening's dinner dance kept racing through his head.

He had thought he might be able to start his life over with Jen. After the way she had looked at him, with her eyes filled with hurt and tears before she stomped off to find her own transportation home, his chances with her were probably slim to none. *Women like Jen Fleming don't hand out second chances.*

Finally, he closed the paper, slammed it on the sofa next to him, and tossed his bifocals on to the coffee table. He rubbed his eyes and dragged his fingers through his hair until his hands rested with his fingers laced at the nape of his neck. He stared at the tiny, blue flicker of flames dancing between the charred logs in the fireplace.

This used to easier. Back in the seventies, when the Eagles were playing on the radio and Barbara was snuggling against me in my 1971 Ford pick-up. He smiled at the memory. He could still smell the sweet scent of her long blonde hair. *She was a beauty.* He saw that natural beauty in Kate. *She's so much like her mother—so very much like Barbara. The woman that filled my soul, the woman I miss everyday.*

It had been ten years since Barbara was killed by a drunk driver—his very own older brother. John was still in Albion State Prison for killing her. Eric was left to raise two of their three children on his own. Thank the Lord for Mike.

Mike was twenty-three at the time. Rife with despair over the untimely loss of the mother that he was so close to, he did what had to be done. He dug right in to help with Shane and Kate.

Kate was sixteen and full of wide-eyed teenaged girl fantasies. God, she needed her mom, but she was stuck with Dad. He did the best he could.

Eric smiled. *Kate turned out terrific despite my lack of motherly instinct.*

Then, there was Shane. Full of piss and vinegar at thirteen, he was already quite the lady's man. *Whew, that was the one that gave me and Mike a run for our money. Sometimes, he still does.*

Yeah, they're grown now.

Eric was ready to pursue a life of his own; maybe with Jen, maybe not. She wasn't answering her phone. She wasn't in her office when he had stopped by twice. She wasn't responding to the messages he had left her. She wasn't giving him a chance to talk it out with her.

Yep, it looks like our relationship has crashed and burned. Damned to hell.

He exhaled hard. He had a mind to drive right over to her place and pound on her door until she let him in. *Not exactly sure what that would accomplish, but it's becoming the viable option, damn it.* He scrubbed a hand over his mouth while seriously giving that option a whirl.

Shane plopped down on the chair across from him and jogged him out of his thoughts. Placing his soda on the coffee table, Shane tossed him an ornery grin while he munched on a ham sandwich. "Sorry to hear you got dumped last night."

Eric sat up. "I didn't get dumped."

"What would you call it? When a date wants to find her own way home, you've been dumped." He grabbed the soda and took a quick swig. "And when you can't contact her—Oh yeah, you've been dumped. And then—"

Wincing, he gestured for him to stop with his hand. "Thank you, Shane. I've got the idea."

Kate walked into the room just as the phone on the desk began to ring. She grabbed it. "Hello ..." She listened before handing the receiver to her father. "Dad, I think it's Margie."

Eric jumped from the sofa and dashed to the desk. With a braced breath, he took the phone from Kate's hand. "Hello ..."

Margie's voice was hesitant but strong. "Eric, it's Margie, are you busy after morning workouts tomorrow?"

Exchanging glances, Kate and Shane watched while apprehension filled their father's face. "I don't know, Margie—"

"Please, Eric," she pleaded with a soft reassuring tone.

"What's up?"

"Reading and writing, like always, at the picnic table under the tree. Please come, Eric."

He could hear a hint of anxiety in her cajoling. "I'll be there." He replaced the phone on its base. He turned to find wary expressions on his children's faces.

"You're going?" Kate was worried that her father was walking into the lion's den without a chair or a whip.

With a shake of his head, Eric leaned a hip against the desk. "I must be a glutton for punishment."

Sinking back into the sofa, Shane chuckled and took another bite of his sandwich.

C3   80   C3   80

When Margie hung up the phone, she felt a tug at her heart. *What a mess I've made of my relationship with Eric.* She was ashamed that she had let Ava convince her that he had deep-hidden feelings for her.

If she were being truthful, she couldn't deny that there was a sputter of attraction on her part for Eric. With the same thick, dark hair, except for a sprinkle of gray, he was an older version of his son. She could see the same mystery in his eyes that she had always observed in Mike's. *Hey, who wouldn't be attracted to that?*

After she had taken the bait and allowed herself to believe that he was secretly in love with her, she fell into the chasm of those feelings for him. *What a fool I made of myself.* When she closed her eyes, she could still see the shock and then the pity, on the Wests' faces, especially Mike's. It still made her gut wrench when she thought of it.

She promised Mike that she would talk to his father. He was right. She did owe Eric more than the cold shoulder that she had been tossing his direction. She had been treating him terribly unfair. By teaching her how to read and write, he had opened a new world for her, as promised. *Sometimes that world is a cold, harsh place; but, thanks to Eric, I'm now better equipped to handle anything it throws at me.*

Tomorrow, they would meet again at the picnic table under the canopy of the big old maple tree. She supposed people would pass by, some would wave and call out to them, and some would stop and watch them. *They'll be more suspicious than ever after everything that's happened.*

Looking around the kitchen, her gaze fell upon her baking pans, flour, sugar, and measuring spoons resting on the table. She wanted to bake something really special. She smiled to herself. Eric West was a very special man.

છ ৪৩ ৩ ৪৩

Jen tossed in her bed. *How many times have I rolled over to check the time? It's now two a.m.* If things had gone according to her carefully, calculated plans, she wouldn't be in this bed alone. Eric would be between these blue sheets and he'd be hers … forever.

Tell God your plans … listen to him laugh.

Tomorrow, she would see Eric. Maybe she should have responded to his messages that he had left on her voice mail, but she'd rather talk to him face-to-face. Hopefully, end with lips-to-lips. She wanted him to forgive her so badly. After the terrible cat fight that she had with Margie in the ladies room that he had to break-up, she felt like she had more than used up all of her chances with him. She wasn't so sure that a man like Eric West gave out more than one chance. She wasn't so sure that she blamed him.

She rolled over toward the window and watched the moon's ray's filter through the curtains to fill the room with a soft ashen glow. *It's going to be a long night.* A tear trickled down her cheek to moisten her pillow.

"Everything will look better in the morning," her mother used to say to her while stroking her hair when she was a young girl filled with angst over a math test or a report she had to deliver in front of a class.

Trying to bite back the tears, she closed her eyes. "Everything will look better in the morning," quietly she repeated her mother's words to herself. She hoped and prayed that her mother would be right just one more time.

⚬ ⚬ ⚬ ⚬

Eric kept checking his watch.

The morning was dragging even though they were busy with a visit from Tom Mason and Colette Beardmore. On alert, the West clan kept a vigilant eye on the pair. They paid particular attention to the location of their vehicles at all times. Kate had driven in to the track with Shane. She wasn't taking any chances with her new Mustang. Calling her a coward, Shane goaded her. She had no problem ignoring him.

Tom was exuberant. He couldn't wait to watch his grand gelding, Ivan, work-out one last time before the big race on Saturday.

Mike was quite pleased with Ivan, who had trained like a champion. He felt confident that the gelding would make an exciting showing at the race.

Waiting anxiously for Ivan to pass with the exercise rider aboard, they stood along the rail. Mike let Tom hold the stopwatch and press the button when Ivan whizzed passed like Bob Baffert working one of his Kentucky Derby hopefuls. The time on the half-mile work was forty-seven seconds, which was the fastest work on the racetrack roster for the morning.

God bless him. Tom gleefully led Ivan back to barn. His chest puffed with pride and excitement for the upcoming race, he told everyone they bumped into about Ivan's workout results. He insisted upon helping cool-out his lean mean racing machine, and Colette offered to get a bucket of water for him. After filling the bucket to overflowing, she struggled to tote it down the aisle toward Mike, Tom, and Ivan.

Mike saw her teetering back and forth with the full bucket. He braced himself for the big splash that would surely happen when she reached him.

He had no problem picturing the scenario: Coco/Colette would trip over her feet to splash the bucket of ice cold water down the front of him—the crotch area, of course, to make it look like he'd peed himself, which would force him to walk around the track looking that way until it dried. *Oh, I'll get quite a teasing from Dan Quaide, Doug O'Conner, Doc Spears, and, naturally, Shane.*

I can hear the comments already, "Hey, Mike, the men's room is at the end of the shed row." "They've got medication for that problem, ya know." "Keep it in your pants, West." Ba-ha-ha-ha-ha!

Nice, real nice.

With that sweet innocent smile on those plump delicious lips, she drew closer and closer still. Tom kept chattering at him, but he didn't hear a word. Bracing for the cool shower he was surely about to receive, he winced. She walked passed him and set the bucket down in front of Ivan. She patted his neck while he took a sip.

Glancing down at his dry jeans, Mike exhaled.

Colette definitely was the "new and improved" version of Coco Beardmore. The blonde klutz that was once painfully plagued with Calamity Jane Syndrome seemed to have climbed out of that chasm.

Eric insisted upon walking Tom and Colette to their vehicle. Where they were concerned, it had become policy, anyway. Mike was proud and quick to point out that the couple's visit was a true success in every-way. Ivan had turned in a winning time, and no disastrous debacles had occurred. It was most impressive, indeed.

After the dynamic duo had been sent safely on their way, Eric glanced at his watch again while holding the lead to a horse that Shane was rubbing-down with liniment.

Shane stood back to study the horse's knee. "Hopefully, the swelling will soon go down." He wiped his hands with a rag.

"It's looking better. He seems sounder on it today." Eric handed the lead to Shane.

He could see the edginess in his father. "You going to see Margie?"

"On my way now." Eric glanced at his watch for the hundredth time while walking toward the barn door.

"Dad ..." Shane called to him. Eric turned. "Margie's not so mangy anymore ... thanks to you."

That urged a smile from Eric. With a nod at his son, he walked out the door.

ɔ ꙅ ɔ ꙅ

The pigeons wobbled and warbled around Eric while he walked through the shed rows. *Perhaps Margie should find another tutor. I don't know how we're going to get past the tension that has been set in motion over the last few weeks.*

His thoughts drifted to Jen. *How am I going to patch things up with her? Enough. After I see Margie, I'll go to Jen's office to iron things out and if she's not there, it's time to go pound on her door—Hell, kick it in if I have to.*

He had weighed his viable options. Now he made his decision. *Game on.*

"Hey, Eric." Dan Quaide's voice jarred him back into the moment. He was walking toward him with a coffee in his hand and a sleazy grin on his face. "I saw Margie sitting at the picnic table about fifteen minutes ago. I think she's waiting on you. Man, she just doesn't give up, does she? She wants it bad, Eric. Why don't you give it to her?" He slapped him on the back.

Enough.

Eric clenched his fist, hauled back, and slammed Dan in the nose. Dan fell to the pavement. His coffee spilled over his chest and blood spewed from his nostrils. Eric stepped over the brawny man and continued toward the old maple tree near the track.

When he rounded the corner of the last stable in the shed row, his eyes widened. Indeed, Margie was waiting at the picnic table for him, but she wasn't alone. She was passing out pencils and tablets to five young Hispanic stable hands.

What the hell?

He went through the gate and across the grass to arrive at the end of the table under the shade of the tree. Smiling, Margie looked up at him while placing a pile of easy readers in the middle of the table. She uncovered a heaping plate of raisin oatmeal cookies. She remembered that they were his favorites, and that hers were much like the ones his late wife used to bake for him.

"Thanks for coming, Eric. I knew you would," Margie said. "I've brought some friends along who want to learn to read." She could see the uneasiness in his rigid stance. "I told them what a good teacher you are, but I also told them what a busy man you are."

Eric took in the caramel-colored faces that were looking back at him. Their dark eyes seemed to be pleading with him. "Margie, I don't know ..."

"I told Margie that I would help."

Jen's voice took him by surprise. He turned to find her leaning against the tree. Her arms were crossed under her breasts. God, she was a sight with her lovely brunette hair wisped around her chin, those big brown eyes, and her pixie-like appearance.

Damn, she always looks so good.

He let go of a breath that he felt he had been holding in his lungs for two days. *Maybe there is a chance for us, after all.*

"Jen and me—"

"Jen and I," Eric corrected her.

Margie sighed. "Jen and I ironed things out between us yesterday."

He swept his hand over his mouth. "No more cat fights in the bathroom?"

Margie rolled her eyes. "Get over yourself, Eric."

Trying to smother a giggle, Jen cleared her throat. "Or maybe you could give what time you can spare to help us help these people."

Eric smiled. "A literacy program, right here at the track ..."

"It was Margie's idea." Jen smiled at her. "I'm willing to volunteer. Margie's willing to organize."

"I want to volunteer, too." Another voice interrupted the persuasion. Scott Carter took a seat next to Margie and tossed her a coy smile. He looked at Jen with a thin smile that was filled with apology and regret.

Eric and Jen exchanged pleased glances. Their eyes flew open wide when Doug O'Conner plodded through the grass to plunk down at the end of the table. He snatched a tablet and a pencil, and spewed a stream of tobacco juice into the grass.

"We really need this, Eric. What do you say?" Margie wheedled.

He looked into the young Hispanic faces and the old weathered face of a man that had hidden his illiteracy for over fifty years. Then, he looked into Margie's eyes, and Jen's. He plucked a raisin oatmeal cookie from the plate and took a bite.

"I say ... let's get started."

Cindy McDonald

~ *Epilogue* ~
Forgive and ... Forget?

Colette wiped a tear from her eye. It was the day of Tom's big race. She was feeling very emotional. Feeling proud of his big gelding, Ivan, and the terrific job that Mike had done training him for this day; Henry Snodgrass, her ex-husband, crept into her mind.

She remembered, how Henry had brought her to the races, had taught her how to read a racing form, and how to make an "educated" choice. She wasn't here with Henry today.

Today was about Tom.

She tugged on her pink and black wide-brimmed hat that matched her black sheath dress, and hot pink Jimmy Choo stilettos.

Today was also the last time she would see Mike West, her gentlemanly cowboy.

She and Tom were going to live in his penthouse in Manhattan. Tom was already talking marriage. Colette was intent on taking their time. Mike had made arrangements with a trainer to take over the management of Ivan at Belmont.

She was going to miss her cowboy. His gorgeous hazel eyes, his buff body, and the way his Levis clung to his oh, so sexy buttocks. *I would've liked to take that cowboy for a little ride. But, it wasn't meant to be,* she contentedly surmised.

Tom was more to her comfort. For some strange reason, she liked the company of older men. Standing along the rail, Tom pulled her close to him when Punch McMinn led Ivan into the paddock at Keystone Downs. She took in the pride that was swelling in Tom's chest, and the anticipation of the race to come.

Mike noticed them at the rail. Smiling, he walked to them. "He's a force to be reckoned with, Tom."

"He looks fantastic, Mike." Colette tugged him to her and kissed his cheek, which left a pink lipstick imprint behind.

He urged a gentle smile. *Hot little ballerina, I'm gonna miss her.*

"Only ten minutes to post," Tom noted. "We'd better find a good spot in the grand stands. We'll catch you there, Mike."

CB ✠ CB ✠

Ten minutes seemed like ten hours to Tom Mason. He fidgeted in the grand stands like an anxious little boy at Mass on Christmas Eve. Suddenly, he felt the strong clap of Eric's hand on his shoulder. He was relieved to turn and see his old friend.

"He's going off five to one. Not bad," Eric duly noted. "I hear congratulations are in order. When's the wedding, Colette?"

Colette tossed Tom an arched look. "Tom-Tom," she scolded before turning back to Eric. "We'll see. Maybe in a year." When Tom's eyes widened, she added, "or two."

Eric chuckled. *This may very well be the woman that keeps Tom Mason in line. Who would have ever guessed?*

"The horses are entering the starting gate," the announcer proclaimed.

Tom whipped his binoculars into place. The flush to his face started at his neck, and slowly burned upward. He tapped his foot against the pavement, and his fingers against the binoculars, as if he were counting each horse being loaded into their post position.

Grinning keenly, Mike stepped up behind them.

The gates sprung open, and the Thoroughbreds leapt from their posts. Ivan stumbled, but the jockey gathered him up, and sent him chasing the pack.

Aware that Ivan now had plenty of real estate to travel to catch the lead horse, Mike's grin faded.

Tom's face became more flushed, his foot tapped frantically, and his fingers tightened around the binoculars. "Damned to hell." he cursed.

"The number six horse, Call Me CJ, has a firm lead rolling into the turn," the announcer called out. "Number four, Ivan, had a stumble start, but is making up ground, directly."

"Bring him home, bring him home," Mike urged.

"Down the stretch they come. Call Me CJ five lengths in front; number two, All Geared Up, is coming on strong; but here comes Ivan stealthily along the rail," the announcer's voice was coming to pique.

The photographer's camera flashed and the crowd cheered when Call Me CJ crossed the finish line as the victor. All Geared Up followed by a length. Ivan had managed an impressive third after coming from behind the stampede.

"Call Me CJ wins comfortably," the announcer shouted before clicking off the microphone.

Colette stiffened. Mike held his breath. With a glowing smile on his face, Tom lowered the binoculars. "Impressive, Mike, quite impressive indeed." He grabbed Mike's hand and shook it feverishly. He grabbed Colette, folded her tightly against him and kissed her neck like a hungry vampire.

Over Tom's shoulder, she spotted Henry a short distance away. Wearing his old trusty binoculars around his neck and a smile on his face, he nodded at her and touched his fingers to his brow, as if he were tipping his hat, before disappearing into the crowd.

CB SO CR ED

Eric walked Tom and Colette to their car. Tom could hardly contain his excitement. Eric thought he was going to break into a skip at any moment.

When Eric held the door of the Porsche open for Colette, she kissed him on the cheek. "Thank you for everything, Mr. West, especially your patience." She slid into the passenger's seat. "And will you please tell Kate that I am truly sorry about her car?"

"Be happy, Coco ... Colette," Eric said, with a wink and a smile.

The banana bread baking in the oven sent a heavenly waft through Margie's kitchen.

She had carried the old battered box of her mother's romance books into the room and set them on a chair. Carefully, one by one, she laid them on the table. She read each title slowly. The corners were brown and bent. Some of the books had been nibbled at by mice. The pictures of the erotic lovers on the covers were faded, but they were a beautiful mystery to her. The romance books were all she had of her mother after she had abandoned Margie and her father many years before.

The kitchen door opening and slamming shut broke through her concentration. Looking up, she found Doug staring at her and the box of books on the chair. She could see the seething burn in his eyes.

He said nothing. Frowning, he stomp to the sink, washed his hands, and dried them on a towel while studying her.

Indifferent to the resentment she could feel permeating from his gaze, she continued to sort through the books and arrange them on the table.

Pitching the dish towel to the counter, he clomped into his bedroom and slammed the door behind him. She could hear him rummaging around the room, banging dresser drawers, and plodding about like an angry child sent to time-out. His bedroom door whipped open to push a gusty draft through the room. Wearing a flushed, tight expression on his weathered face, he marched to the kitchen and slapped an old photograph face down on the table.

Her questioning wary eyes met his. When he withdrew his hand from the photo, he shot her a "go ahead" nod before going out the kitchen door.

After the slam, Margie leaned against the counter to stare at the photograph on the table. With a braced breath and a deep swallow, she reached for the picture. Her heart thrummed against her chest when she turned it over. Tears swelled in her eyes while she studied the face of the mother she had no recollection of.

There she was. Tall and thin with long brunette hair that was just like Margie's. She was no raving beauty, either. *Pity, I've always imagined her looking like a movie star. That's why she didn't want or couldn't stay with dad and me. Her beauty was too grand to waste on this beat-up old farm. That wasn't the case. She was as homely as me.*

Margie strained to study the grainy image of her mother holding her daughter on her hip while smiling into the camera. *Funny, she doesn't look unhappy at all in this drab old picture.* Slowly, she turned it over. There was an address on the back. Denver, Colorado.

 C3 ⁞ C3 ⁞

Carrying a plate of warm banana bread, Margie stepped out of the kitchen door onto the small unkempt back porch. The cinnamon butter melted over the steaming aromatic bread. Her father leaned against the porch post with his hands tucked into the pockets of his worn-out flannel pants. He stared out at the old Thoroughbreds mulling about behind the baler twine fence. He seemed meditative and sad.

Doug spit tobacco into the bristly weeds beyond the porch. There was nothing genteel or tender about Doug O'Conner. He was a hard man, with a hard heart that seemed to have softened … maybe just a little.

"That's as good as it gets, Marge. That's the last address I had for your mom. She wrote me four years after she left. She wanted to see you. Screw her. She left. She had no right—not no more," he said, bitterly. He turned and she offered him the plate of piping hot bread. "You patch things up with Scott?"

"Mostly." Margie watched him savor the taste of the cinnamon and the banana.

"Suppose you'll be leaving me, too."

"Naw, who'd put up with you, anyways?" Margie chuckled while urging a tiny curl from his craggy lips.

"You gonna look for her?" he asked in probably the softest tone she'd ever heard from him.

"Maybe, I got some thinking to do." She did something that she had never done before. She wrapped her arms around her father and rested her head on his shoulder.

The old coot seemed to like it.

CB EO CR EO

Strong black coffee, that's what Lugowski had a taste for. McDonald's coffee never tasted as good as that afternoon when he sipped it with Kate West, the blue-eyed blonde that had his brain wrangled in a tight ball of confusion.

It was that very confusion that had made him break protocol by convincing Captian Lutz to let him interrogate Margie O'Conner. Being a by-the-book kind of man, he was shocked when the captain gave him the nod. Maybe Lutz enjoyed pissing-off Detective Steward as much as Lugowski enjoyed doing the deed.

After Margie's release, he jokingly told Kate that she owed him. *Jokingly? So why am I steering my SUV through the stone entrance of Westwood Thoroughbred Farm?* Coffee and Kate. At the moment, they seemed like a tasty combination.

The grand Victorian style farmhouse was peeking through the tangle of branches of gracious oaks lining the driveway. He slowed the SUV to a stop in front of the house and stared at the steering wheel. Mechanically, he flipped an unlit cigarette through his fingers. Oh yeah, he wanted to light that sucker up.

C'mon. I finally have the woman I've wanted all my life. Ava. I wanted her before she was Ava West. I wanted her the entire time she was married to Mike. Now she's exactly where I want her to be—in my life—and in my bed.

Again, he found himself wrestling with the same question: *What the hell am I doing in Kate's driveway? No argument, the girl stirs me. The girl has sass. The girl's a keeper. She's also Mike West's little sister and Ava's ex-sister-in-law. How out of the ball park is that?*

Ava would rip me apart ten ways from Sunday, if she knew where I was. Correction: Ava would break it off with me, and probably go running back to Mike. How cozy would that be? Ava with Mike and me with Kate—not reality—but hey, crazier things have happened. Whoa, not that I want to be with Kate, right? Shit. I should throw the damned vehicle into reverse, and get the hell outta here before—

Tap.

Tap.

Tap.

Kate lightly rapped her knuckles on his window. *Too late.* He let the window down. She looked at him, bemused, with those beautiful, sensual, blue eyes that were the core of his confusion, stimulation, and straight-up trepidation.

"Hey, Carl, what's going on? Am I under arrest?" She laughed.

God help me. I'd like to arrest her. I'd like to take her in my arms, feel the curve of her body against mine, kiss her, taste every inch of her, and try like hell to satisfy whatever it is that she stirs inside of me. Instead, he dragged his gaze to hers, and with that boyish smirk unconsciously planted on his lips, he proceeded with the truth.

"I'm here to collect."

The End

Cindy McDonald

A Note From The Author

I hope you have enjoyed reading *Hot Coco* as much as I enjoyed writing it for you. The Unbridled stories are fiction. That said, there are pieces of my life experiences weaved into the storylines, small reminders of what was going on at the time of writing the book. Included within the anecdotes are situations, exaggerated upon, of course, that have actually happened. Example: The burning down of Coco's kitchen— *Almost* a true story—enough said. ;}

Many of the Thoroughbreds mentioned in *Hot Coco* are horses that have actually raced for our stable, Salty Silver Sally, Call Me CJ, and the mischievous Charlatan.

Thank you for reading *Hot Coco*. I love to write these stories and I have many more to share. I invite you to read the following excerpt from the next book of the Unbridled Series ...

Cindy McDonald

Dangerous Deception

The fading sunlight seeped through the curtains to shimmer over the silky white Persian cat, Stella, sleeping on the window sill. The flickering candles on the vanity sent a waft of vanilla throughout the room to camouflage the smell of sex.

Ava West's auburn hair cascaded across her shoulders. Her breathing was shallow and steady against Carl Lugowski's chiseled chest.

Lieutenant Carl Lugowski worked homicide for the Rosemount Police Department. He was normally a light sleeper, as most cops are. Subconsciously, they must always be prepared for that emergency phone call from the station to jolt them from their bed because a body had been found in some dark alley or a domestic argument had gone terribly awry to result in murder.

Today, Carl's gentle snore was restful while holding Ava's beautiful naked body in his arms. After their afternoon of abandoned love-making, his sleep was deep.

God, she knew how to get to him. He had taken a half day off. They were supposed to see a matinee, but when he arrived at her apartment, Ava had other plans. Not a problem. Nosiree, Bob. She answered the door in a dark blue lace teddy that accentuated the swell of her round breasts and her stiff nipples peeking through the sheer delicate fabric. Her sultry green eyes had a "come on" look. Her plump lips curled. They were begging to be kissed hard.

Ava didn't flirt. When she wanted sex, she was shameless.

She had opened the door and pressed her lips to his. While running her hands over his chest and unbuttoning his shirt, there was no fumbling. The buttons slipped open with unerring precision.

He slipped the strap of the teddy from her shoulder to bare her beautiful breast. Running his tongue over the pebbled nipple, he felt the undeniable pressure of his erection.

When she pushed him away, her smile turned devious.

Ava was like that. She teased.

He knew what she was about.

As gracefully as a dancer, she swooped up two glasses of wine from the hall table and strutted toward the bedroom. Her long silky hair caressed her back as she moved.

Lord have mercy, how he loved to watch her walk toward that bedroom where pleasure would rule the afternoon, and where once would never be enough to satisfy her desire. Ava was a demanding lover, and he aimed to please and please and freaking please.

Who needs a damned movie?

Their clothes lie on the floor, and the daylight was gently giving way to the purple whisper of twilight. They were spent.

The sheets lightly covered their warm moist naked bodies, until suddenly the surreal quiet was broken by Lugowski's cell phone buzzing and vibrating against the lamp on the nightstand. *Damn it.* His eyes dragged open slowly and rotated toward the meddling reverberation. Letting out a low grouse, he begrudgingly reached for the phone. Ava tugged at his arm.

"Let it go to voice mail," she murmured.

Not a bad idea. In fact, he was seriously considering it, when his eyes caught the name on the screen: KATE WEST.

Game changer.

His relationship with Ava meant the world to him. He had wanted that woman since well, forever. He wanted her when they were in high school. He wanted her while he was away at the academy, and he still wanted her when he returned to find that she was Mike West's wife. But now she was exactly where he always wanted her to be, in his life, and in his bed.

Wrangled and rocked beyond his control, his heart helplessly skipped a beat when Kate West was around; hell, when Kate West's name was merely mentioned. She stirred something inside him that he couldn't explain. He couldn't wrap his head around it. It confused and, quite frankly, scared the hell out of him.

She wasn't the clichéd blue-eyed, blonde-haired, "girl next door". But she was definitely a woman any man would want to come home to, wrap his arms around, and make love to night after night. Kate West was what Lugowski would define as "a keeper".

WTF? He was in bed with the woman of his dreams. He should really let the call go. *Yeah, really, that's what I should do.* She was squeezing him. *Why would she be calling? We don't have anything but a professional relationship. So ...*

"I need to take this. Sorry, baby." Sitting up, he pressed the phone as tightly and as covertly as possible to his ear. "Lugowski ..." He made sure he sounded authoritative and official.

"Carl, I'm so sorry to bother you. This is Kate West."

Dragging her fingers through her hair, Ava perked her ears when she detected a slightly familiar female voice filtering through the receiver. It made her brows furrow and her lips purse. Suspicion was mixing it up with jealousy—fast. While Lugowski had muffled the voice, she tilted her head against the pillow, narrowed her eyes, and became engaged.

The voice sounded like Kate's, and that was definitely an unacceptable intrusion on her afternoon delight.

"What's going on?" Lugowski recognized the disquiet in her voice.

"I don't want to talk about it over the phone, but it's really important, Carl. Can we meet at McDonald's?"

Coffee. He had had coffee with the lovely blonde at McDonald's several times. Usually it was at his request. It had become almost a code between them—never anything sexual, and he wasn't sure what he would do if it ever did. *Shit. What am I thinking? Kate is Mike West's little sister, and Ava's ex-sister-in-law. It's too complicated, too weird, too out-of-control ...*

"I'm on my way." No hesitation. The words spilled right out of his mouth. He ended the call, pitched the sheets aside, swung his legs over the bed, and reached for his boxer briefs.

Briskly sitting up, Ava grabbed his arm. The black satin sheets slipped to her waist. Her breasts bobbed delicately into glorious view. "What? Wait a minute. Where are you going?" she demanded in a high-pitched annoyed tone.

It only took a nanosecond for her green bedroom eyes to morph into a jaded glower.

It was a justified question that he couldn't give an honest answer to, unless he was absolutely sure he wanted to endure the repercussions. Ava would be furious, to say the least, if she knew he was leaving her bed to go to Kate's aid, or whatever it was that he was going to. He wasn't sure.

He only knew he had to go.

About the Author

For the past twenty years, Cindy has helped her husband raise, train, and race Thoroughbreds at their forty-five acre farm known as Fly-By-Night Stables near Pittsburgh.

During those years, Cindy has paid close attention to the characters that hang-out at the back-side of the track. She found the situations and life style most intriguing. In 2005, she sat down at her computer and began a journey into writing about this life that few understand.

Cindy has recently retired from making her living as a professional choreographer. She owned and operated Cindy McDonald's School of Dance since 1985. She studied at Pittsburgh Ballet Theatre School and with the Pittsburgh Dance Alloy at Carnegie Mellon University to name a few. She has choreographed many musicals and an opera for the Pittsburgh Savoyards.

To find out more about future books of the Unbridled Series, please visit Cindy's website at: www.cindymcwriter.com

Also Available From
The UnBridled Series

Make a note: never agitate a madman. Successful Thoroughbred trainer Mike West just made that mistake, and he's gonna pay-more than he ever realized. But it's all in the family; his sister, Kate, has been the object of the madman's desire on the social network site "My Town". Her constant rejections have infuriated him. People who seem to be in his way start turning up dead, and he's got Kate and Mike next on his list! In the first book of The Unbridled Series Cindy McDonald introduces you to the world of Thoroughbred racing, while taking her cast of characters for a wild ride through a maniac's mind.

www.ingramcontent.com/pod-product-compliance
Lightning Source LLC
Chambersburg PA
CBHW060051260626
47160CB00005B/1649